Sinner

MIDNIGHT GODS BOOK II

LILAH LANCE

Midnight Gods Book II

Sinner

To the girl who wanted more but didn't know how to ask
I hope the Universe gave it to you

Content Warning

This book contains and may contain mentions of

- Miscarriages
- Domestic violence
- Child abuse
- Explicit content
- Explicit scenes and graphic language
- Violence and abuse

CHAPTER 1
Natasha

I woke up screaming.

Again.

It was always two a.m.

Like clockwork.

As if my body had memorized the hour hell cracked open.

The scream tore out of my throat before I was fully awake, raw and ragged, ripping through the darkness of my room like a blade.

My sheets were soaked, tangled around my limbs like restraints I hadn't agreed to.

I sat up in bed, panting, heart thundering in my ears.

Then came the metal.

Screeching, sharp, violent.

The sound of a car door being torn from its hinges. A crash that lived inside my bones.

Glass shattered next—spraying into the void of my memory like confetti in a graveyard.

It never changed.

The nightmare always started the same way.

But I never knew how it would end.

I was in that place again.

That disoriented, suspended state.

The one where time bent and my thoughts blurred, where I couldn't tell if what I was feeling was real…or just some broken echo of the past.

Was it happening to me?

Around me?

Inside me?

My brain couldn't decide.

My body didn't care.

It reacted anyway—trembling, drenched in sweat, my lungs straining to catch breath that refused to stay.

In that liminal space, the world felt muffled.

Muted, like the static of an old television left on in an empty house.

But even in that numbness, one sound always broke through.

Laughter.

Her laughter.

It sliced through everything.

Clear, sharp, cruel.

I could still hear it, even now.

Like it had been stitched into the fabric of my nightmares.

Not warm or maternal.

But cold. Twisted.

Triumphant.

My mother.

No.

Not that word.

Don't give her that.

I could hear my therapist's voice inside my head, low and steady, trying to pull me back.

"Camilla Delacroix is not your mother, Natasha. You don't have to call her that."

Because mothers didn't hold pillows over their daughters' faces.

Mothers didn't tell eight-year-olds that they were mistakes.

That they should've died in the womb.

Mothers didn't laugh while pressing their heel into their child's throat.

Camilla Delacroix wasn't a mother.

She was a monster.

A devil with red lipstick and expensive perfume.

She wore designer guilt and a smile so rehearsed it belonged on a stage.

Even now, I could see her in the dark.

Standing at the foot of my bed.

Grinning like she knew I'd never be free of her.

She haunted me.

Not like a ghost.

But like a disease I hadn't survived.

I remembered the way she sneered at me in the hospital after the incident—

as if I had ruined her evening by not dying.

Some people were born to be parents.

Like my sister, Talia, who had warmth in her hands and a spine made of gold.

And some people were born to break things.

To burn the world around them and call it love.

Camilla had been the latter.

And I? I was her collateral damage.

An accident. A failed abortion.

A child she never wanted, never loved.

She used to tell me,

"The pill didn't work. And neither did you."

My name was Natasha Delacroix for the first eleven years of my life.

Until Malcolm Nash adopted me.

He took me in when he saw what she was capable of.

He said he'd protect me.

And for a while, I believed him.

But protection came with its own price.

And affection has teeth when it's conditional.

I have mixed feelings about Malcolm.

Because he was my adoptive father.

Until last year.

When I killed him.

And then, I killed Camilla.

Sort of.

I lay back down slowly, the sheets now cold against my skin, my breath slowing to something like stillness. But the room didn't feel empty.

It never did.

The shadows moved over me—shifting, curling, whispering.

They slithered across the walls like they had a purpose.

Like they knew my name.

Like they were waiting.

I stared at the ceiling, eyes wide open, trying not to blink.

Trying not to remember.

But memory is a trick mirror.

You think you're in control until the glass breaks.

And suddenly, you're that girl again.

The one she tried to kill.

The one he tried to control.

The one no one wanted.

I wondered, not for the first time,

if the monsters I killed ever truly died.

Or if they just climbed inside me instead.

And somewhere between the crushing weight of the steering wheel and my mother's hysteric laughter, I feel death hovering—not mine, but someone else's. Always someone else's.

Some people count sheep to fall asleep. I count the dead who visit me.

The shadow shifts—not toward me, but toward the window where Hong Kong's neon lights paint the midnight sky in artificial dawn.

My hands shake as I reach for my phone. 3:33 AM. Of course.

I'm not sure if I'm apologizing for Malcolm or for all the other deaths that cling to the Nash legacy like tar.

Art security sounds clean on paper. Preserving beauty, protecting history. No one talks about the bodies that pile up when millions of dollars of art exchange hands in the dark.

Forty-three days of running Nash Group from hotel rooms because the Hong Kong office felt safer than New York.

Forty-three days of wondering if she'd ever forgive me for what I had to do.

I swing my legs over the bed, fingers automatically reaching for my cane.

The sterling silver handle, carved with protection runes by the shaman I met in Thailand, feels cool against my palm.

My ankle screams as I stand—a familiar song of scar tissue and metal pins that never quite healed right. Mother made sure of that.

"Miss Nash?" A knock at my door. "Your private jet is ready whenever you'd like to depart."

I look at my reflection in the window.

A ghost stares back—platinum hair wild from nightmare sweat, blue eyes rimmed red from another sleepless night.

I may be twenty-one, may run one of the biggest security firms in the world, but in this moment I feel eight years old again, trapped in that car as my mother explained all the ways she planned to kill me.

But Talia needs me.

And for her—for the sister who saved me when blood family tried to destroy me—I'll face any darkness.

Even my own.

"I'll be down in twenty minutes," I call back, already reaching for the Givenchy suit I laid out last night. "Tell the pilot to file a flight plan for New York."

The dead can follow me across oceans. But for once, I'm flying toward life instead of running from death.

I jolt awake in sheets that cost more than most people's monthly rent, my right ankle throbbing with phantom pain.

The Hong Kong skyline pierces through floor-to-ceiling windows, but I'm not looking at the city. I'm looking at the shadow standing in the corner of my suite.

It's been exactly forty-three days since I killed Malcolm Nash.

Since I chose Talia over the man who gave me his name but never his love. The shadow in my room looks nothing like him, but I know it's here because of what I did.

Some people count sheep to fall asleep. I count the dead who visit me.

Start in the nightmare itself - fragments of the car accident

Mix in sensory details that blur between past and present

Show her spiritual sensitivity through how she experiences the nightmare

Have her jolt awake in her Hong Kong hotel room, maybe sensing/seeing something others can't

THE PENTHOUSE FEELS TOO BRIGHT, TOO WARM, TOO ALIVE.

The scar on my right ankle is bothering me too much. Just a little too much.

I hover in the doorway, my cane making soft clicks against marble as I shift my weight. Manhattan sprawls behind the floor-to-ceiling windows like a concrete garden, but all I can focus on is how Talia glows as she cradles Drew.

"Come here," she says softly. "He wants to meet his aunt."

His aunt. The words feel like shards of glass in my throat. If I could cut myself open with them to feel something, I would. But I remain a ghost, existing on another plane while Talia radiates life from the white leather couch.

Drew's tiny fist waves in the air, and I think of another hand—Malcolm's—reaching for a gun. The metallic taste of that night floods my mouth.

"Natasha." Talia's voice carries that gentle authority she's always used with me, ever since I was eight and she found me trying to walk without crutches. "Stop hiding in the doorway."

"I'm not hiding." But I am. I'm always hiding. "How are you? Has Andrei...?"

Her face tightens for just a moment. "Still in Hong Kong. Something about a massive art acquisition that couldn't wait. Not even for his son's birth."

Hong Kong. Where I've been for forty-three days. Where I ran after Malcolm. Where Andrei was instead of here.

The coincidence tastes like copper in my mouth.

"You should sit," Talia says, patting the space beside her. "Your ankle must be killing you after the flight."

My ankle always kills me. Mother made sure of that. But I take the offered seat, keeping careful inches between us.

Drew's dark hair marks him as Andrei's son—all that DuPont coloring—but when his eyes open, they're all Talia.

"Do you want to hold him?"

"I'll drop him." The words escape before I can stop them. "I'm not...I'm not steady enough."

"Natasha." Talia's voice breaks a little. "You're the steadiest person I know. You saved my life. You saved *his* life. If you hadn't been there when Malcolm—"

"Don't." The shadows in the corner of the room seem to pulse. "Please."

She studies me for a long moment, then shifts Drew in her arms.

"You know what I see when I look at you? I see the little girl who used to play piano despite her mother saying her hands were too clumsy. I see the teenager who built herself back up after every fall. I see my sister who's somehow convinced herself she's broken when really, she's the strongest person I know."

6

I want to tell her she's wrong. That I'm held together with scar tissue and nightmares. That the dead follow me now, collecting like debt. That sometimes I wake up tasting blood that isn't there.

Instead, I force my lips into what I hope passes for a smile. "He's beautiful, Talia. He has your nose."

She lets me change the subject, but I feel her worry like a physical touch.

"Stay with us for a while. The building has plenty of empty apartments, and I miss you. Drew needs his aunt close by."

Close by. As if proximity could fix what's broken inside me.

As if love alone could erase the fact that I killed her father to save her.

"I have meetings," I lie.

Outside, New York continues its endless sounds of life. In here, I remain suspended between worlds—not quite dead, but not really living either.

Drew made a small sound, and for just a moment, I let myself imagine what it would be like to be whole.

To be the aunt he deserves. To be the sister Talia believed me to be. And I realized I couldn't even imagine it.

I had no idea what she looked like or what she should've felt on the inside other than carved out with an ice-cream scooper.

Empty.

Open.

Desiccated.

And bleeding from the inside out. Begging myself internally somewhat to be fixed from the inside, but unable to figure out how.

But some broken things can't be fixed.

And some ghosts aren't meant to rejoin the living.

And I didn't think I was a worthy fit for anything.

CHAPTER 2
Natasha

I WASN'T AVOIDING MY SISTER.

No.

It had been three months since I saw my nephew.

But Talia was astute.

Talia would always know when something was off or wrong with me. She always did.

Talia was more like my mother than a sibling. If anything at being eight years older than me, I didn't even see her as my real sister. And I know Talia was more doing her duty to me than anything else.

So I wasted away in my room.

Bexley Carter came over sometimes to visit me. Two years younger than me, she came with her shadow a six foot six giant of a man named Garrett Fuller.

He came bearing bagels and snacks and he was pretty chill for a big dude.

Bexley looked comically small next to him in her goth girl get-up with bowls, blonde hair pulled back with more bows and combat boots on her feet. Garrett in comparison carried everything.

"How's life at Titan?"

"Good," she smiled as Garrett put down bagels. "G and I are working a case." Her South African accent was musical as she spoke grinning to me. I didn't know where Bexley came from but she was another stray Talia had picked up over the years.

"Oh?"

"Mhm, we're gonna go investigate, but for now, I thought I'd pop in and make sure you were all right, eh?"

Garrett moved around her putting down things for me including flowers which I thanked him for.

"So what are you doing now? Besides trying to be the next CEO of Nash Group?" Bexley took a bite into her bagel offering me some and I eyed Garrett who carefully sipped his coffee watching her. He even lowered his chair down lower so she could be taller than him.

Every Sunday like clockwork Bexley came over for brunch after she'd assimilated to Titan.

She'd come to New York with my sister's friend Alma and Samara, Talia's shadow. Now, she was walking around with her own shadow perched next to her like a behemoth feeding her bagels.

Like his little bird.

"Do you go outside sometime?" Bexley asked innocently enough. "We can take you out. I like going to the aquarium with Garrett."

Garrett smirked looking down at her. "She likes the sharks."

"They like me. They always stop when they see me."

"That's because they think you're dinner," I muttered. "Has Samara killed her boy toy yet?"

Bexley giggled. "No, Thierry made them work together so now it's driving her crazy."

Samara had gotten herself into a situation.

One with tremendous irony.

"What's her man's name?"

"Shane," Garrett murmured with another smirk.

"How the fuck did that happen? How does she accidentally end up with a Titan?"

Bexley looked up at Garrett who shook his head. "I don't spill."

"Aww, come on. You're the only one who knows how Samara and Shane ended up together."

Garrett took a bite out of his bagel and didn't say anything. When he wasn't mean mugging he was actually relatively handsome.

Green eyes. Blonde hair.

Not my type.

Bexley nudged Garrett with her elbow, eyes gleaming with mischief.

"Aw, come on. You're turning back into the enemy."

Garrett gave her a lazy smile and shook his head. "I didn't think I ever stopped being the enemy."

"Sometimes you're not the enemy."

"Oh yeah? When?"

"When you bring me bagels."

"And ice cream..."

"And donuts..."

A grin tugged at her mouth. "And donuts," she repeated, pleased with herself. "Oh! Can we get donuts after this?"

"Depends." Garrett watched her now, amusement playing at the corners of his mouth. "Am I still the enemy?"

Bexley hesitated, pretending to think it over. "No."

"Then we can get donuts."

I snorted under my breath. "You two are disgustingly cute."

Bexley turned several shades of red while Garrett's smirk deepened.

I didn't say anything more. I rarely did, especially in moments like that—moments that felt too warm, too open. I was more comfortable in silence.

Later, I left the apartment alone, tugging my baseball cap low over my face. My platinum hair slipped out from beneath the brim in wisps, but I didn't bother fixing it. The less anyone saw of me, the better.

Dinner had been my usual—halal chicken and rice, extra white sauce. New York had that down to a science.

I stepped into the elevator, head ducked, shoulders tight. I kept to one corner, adjusting the brim of my cap again as if I could hide behind it. My cane clicked softly against the metal floor. I focused on my breathing. In for four. Hold for four. Out for four.

The chrome walls bounced fragmented reflections back at me—ice-blue eyes, pale skin, hollow cheeks, the tension in my jaw.

I didn't even notice when someone else stepped in until the scent of expensive cologne reached me. Subtle. Sharp. Masculine. The kind of scent worn by people who could afford not to think about price tags.

I shrank further into the corner.

The elevator glided upward. Floor 23...24...25...

Then everything jolted.

The lights flickered once.

Twice.

Then died.

Total darkness slammed into me like a punch.

No.

No no no no no—

A scream tore from my throat before I could stop it.

I wasn't in the elevator anymore. I was eight years old again.

The metal of the car crushed my ankle. The world was sideways. Water filled the cabin. And my mother was laughing. Laughing while I screamed.

My cane slipped from my grip, clattering to the floor as my knees gave out. I folded into the corner, arms shaking, body curling in on itself.

The walls were too close. The air too thin.

Then a voice broke through the panic—low, calm, grounding.

"Hey. You're alright. Just a power fluctuation. Nothing more."

I couldn't see him. Couldn't breathe. My chest heaved and my fingers scrabbled uselessly against the cold wall. I couldn't get out. I couldn't get out—

"Listen to my voice." His tone held authority, but not the kind I was used to. Not sharp, not cruel. Steady. Gentle. "You're in an elevator in Manhattan. It's 2024. You're safe."

A phone flashlight flicked on, cutting through the black. I flinched at the sudden light, but it helped. Just enough to orient myself.

His face came into view in pieces. High cheekbones. Clean-cut jaw. Eyes the same electric blue as mine, but warmer somehow. Like the color held heat instead of ice.

But I couldn't focus on him. My mind was still stuck behind the wheel, in the twisted wreckage of a past I couldn't erase.

"I can't—" My voice cracked. "I can't be in here. I can't—"

He crouched slowly, keeping distance. Not touching. Not forcing. Just...being there.

"Look at me."

I did, barely. My vision was blurred, not from the light but from tears I refused to shed.

"What's your name?"

CHAPTER 3

Teo

CHAPTER 4
Natasha

I WASN'T AFRAID OF THE DARK.

Not exactly.

But trapped in an electrical box in the dark with a man.

"Shhh."

An animal scream left me the moment the lights turned off.

I'd never screamed like that in my life.

And he was on me.

"Shhhhh, mon coeur, shhhh." I couldn't stop freaking out. "No, no, it's okay. It's okay."

I couldn't stop freaking out as another sob left me.

"Shhh…it's okay. It's okay." He brushed my hair back and I felt myself losing my mind a little. I kept seeing the car.

"The car's going to hit us—"

"Nothing's going to hit us—"

"It's coming for me—"

"It's not, I promise—"

"I can see it. She's turning—" I screamed again and again until my voice went out. "Stop! Stop! Stop!"

I had PTSD.

And to my complete shock, I felt him moving, tucking me into his jacket and holding me tightly as the panic grew.

I felt his lips at my ear soothing, calming. I didn't know him, I just knew when I got on, I caught a glimpse of a pretty man and he'd ducked his head.

He was whispering things to me in another language. French? I didn't speak anything but English and Japanese. Talia's mom's language. Talia taught me.

I couldn't stop shaking.

"There is no car. There is just me—"

"What if we die—"

"We don't—"

"How do you know—"

"I just do—"

"What if something happens—"

"Nothing is going to happen—"

"But you don't know that—"

"This elevator isn't going to fall, it's just a minor outage."

"How do you know?"

"I'm an engineer—"

"For elevators—"

"For cars

CHAPTER 5

WAS IT MY STROKE OF LUCK I WAS TRAPPED IN AN ELEVATOR WITH MY neighbor?

Perhaps.

I wouldn't have complained had I not had a meeting to go to.

There was a time I would've leapt at the opportunity to...ask out anyone? No. I didn't ask. I just showed up.

I wasn't good at romance.

And I never pretended to be.

If women were under the illusion I'd send them flowers—that wasn't on me.

I knew exactly who my neighbor was.

Because I make it a point to know who lives around me—and Jace, my personal data bloodhound, makes sure I don't miss a damn thing.

Apartment 11B. Natasha Nash.

Andrei's sister-in-law.

My sister-in-law, technically.

Though I doubted she knew that.

She'd lived next door for three months and hadn't said more than a nod in the hallway.

Quiet. Private. Always moving like she wanted the walls to swallow her whole.

I wasn't used to women like that.

Most women either tried to get close or made a show of ignoring me just long enough to be noticed.

Natasha didn't do either. She simply…existed. Which somehow made her impossible to ignore.

And yet, I stayed away.

Because she was off-limits. Because Andrei had made that clear.

Because something about her made me pause.

And I don't pause for anyone.

Being trapped in an elevator with her?

Not on my list of contingencies. Definitely not in my top five scenarios.

Then I heard it—her voice.

Small. Raw.

"I didn't do anything," she whispered, voice small and broken. Like a child's. "I promise I didn't do anything. It wasn't my fault."

Something in my chest tightened—not with sympathy, but something colder. Rage, maybe. That someone made her believe she had to say that.

"I know you didn't," I said quietly. "It's okay."

"I promise." Her fingers clutched my shirt tighter. "I promise I was good."

"I believe you," I told her, keeping my voice steady even as my jaw locked. Someone had done this to her. Someone had broken her this badly. "You didn't do anything wrong."

Her whole body shook. "I'm—I'm upside down."

Fuck. She wasn't here anymore. She was somewhere else, deep under.

"What do you see?" I asked, shifting to hold her up more securely.

"The car…we crashed. She's—" A sob tore through her throat. "She's just standing there. Texting."

"Who's standing there?" I asked, even though I already knew.

"My mother."

The word dropped between us like acid.

Not *mom*. Not *mama*. Just *mother*. Cold. Clinical. Distant.

I'd heard that tone before—in people who carried trauma like armor. In war rooms. In courtrooms. In interrogation chambers.

I pulled her closer, instinct overriding caution.

"Tu n'es plus là," I murmured. *You're not there anymore.*

"You're here. With me. In New York. In an elevator."

She gasped, still spiraling.

"I need—" Her breath hitched. "I need to call Talia."

I froze. "Who?"

"My sister. She just had a baby. She'll worry—"

Everything inside me stopped.

Talia. Baby. Platinum-blonde hair. Fragile voice.

This wasn't just some woman in distress.

This was Natasha Nash.

My sister-in-law.

The one Andrei told me to stay away from. The one he called *fragile* like it was both a warning and a confession.

She trembled in my arms again, her body still caught between then and now.

"Natasha," I said her name for the first time, gently. "Regarde-moi." *Look at me.*

Her lashes fluttered, her eyes finally beginning to focus.

"You're safe," I told her. "Je te jure." *I swear to you.*

And I meant it.

God help me, I meant it.

She didn't know who I was.

And I couldn't bring myself to tell her.

She trembled against me, lost in the memory, and I needed to pull her back. Now.

"So," I said conversationally, as if we weren't trapped in a dark elevator with her having a panic attack in my arms. "Do you always pounce on strange men in elevators?"

She went completely still. "I did not—"

"I'm teasing—"

"Oh." The word came out small, confused. Like she'd never been teased before.

Her fingers loosened slightly on my shirt.

Her voice cracked like glass under pressure—just enough to let sound through without shattering completely. I didn't move too fast.

Didn't breathe too hard. I was holding something fragile, and one wrong word might leave me picking up pieces I had no right to touch.

"I don't...pounce."

No, I didn't imagine she did.

"No?" I adjusted my hold, letting her settle more comfortably against

17

me. "Because I distinctly remember someone launching herself at me the moment the lights went out."

She made a sound—not quite a laugh, but close. A crack in the ice.

"That's not...that's not what happened."

"You're right. You fell with exceptional grace. Very swan-like."

"Swan-like?" Now there was definitely a hint of laughter in her voice, even if it was watery.

"Would you prefer another animal? Perhaps a startled gazelle? An elegant giraffe?"

She squirmed slightly.

She was still shaking, but less like an earthquake now. More like the after-shock that reminded you what had survived. And all I could do was anchor her. Let her shake. Let the dust settle.

"Are you always this..." she asked slowly.

"Charming? Devastatingly handsome? Good at catching falling women?"

"Ridiculous," she finished, but the panic had ebbed from her voice.

"Only in broken elevators, mon cœur," I murmured. "Only in broken elevators."

Her face turns up toward mine in the harsh phone light, and for a moment, I forget how to breathe. Those eyes—powder blue ringed with darkness—hold galaxies of pain.

The kind of pain that transforms people into either victims or survivors.

I found myself cataloging details with scientific precision: the slight tremble in her lower lip, the constellation of freckles across her nose, the way her pulse races visible in her throat. Beautiful, yes, but it's her fragility that catches me off guard. Makes me want to—

No.

I don't save people.

I don't fix broken things.

I calculate, manipulate, and destroy.

It's what I'm good at. It's what made me a billionaire before thirty.

And yet my thumb traces circles on her shoulder, and I keep talking—stupid, meaningless words about pressure systems and backup genera-tors. Anything to keep her anchored to the present.

She's a stranger. A random woman in a random elevator. Nothing more.

She slowly blinked up at me as I winced covering both of us at it started moving again, this time going down and I held Natasha Nash my fucking sister in law in my arms.

Slowly when the doors opened she tucked herself into me endearingly. My heart cracked open.

This is why Andrei told me to stay away from her.

The doors opened and I saw a dozen people worried on me.

Three things happened at the same time.

"Mr. DuPont—"

"Who's in charge of maintenance?" My voice was steel as everyone paled.

"I am, sir." Someone else stood up.

"You're fired." I just spent forty minutes with crying Natasha in my arms. That was enough.

I looked down at the woman in my arms who was now blinking up at me and I realized just how fucking adorable she was.

"You're...Thierry's brother..."

"Teo," I smiled all teeth. "Nice to meet you."

CHAPTER 6
Natasha

THE WALLS WERE A SOFT, UNTHREATENING GRAY, THE KIND OF COLOR meant to make people open up. But I'd learned that even the gentlest walls could feel like cages when the truth started pressing in.

Becky studied me from her chair, legs crossed neatly, notebook open in her lap. Her pen had stilled.

"You seem...distracted today," she said gently. Not a challenge. Not a prod. Just...an invitation.

I blinked at the floor-to-ceiling window across from me, eyes tracing the edge of a slow-moving cloud.

Still half in that elevator.

Still half in his arms.

Still half in that low, grounding voice whispering, *"Tu n'es plus là."*

"I got stuck in an elevator," I said finally.

Becky didn't react—not a flinch, not a blink. Just a quiet tilt of her head. "Alone?"

I hesitated, my fingers toying with the hem of my sleeve. "No."

Her brows lifted slightly, the way they always did when she wanted me to notice I'd said something I wasn't saying.

"Would you like to talk about it?"

I shrugged. "I mean, we didn't die."

The laugh that followed felt sharp in my throat. Dry. Defensive.

"The lights flickered. I panicked. There was someone else inside."

Becky said nothing. She was good at that—letting silence stretch just long enough to make me fill it.

I sighed. "Matteo DuPont."

That got her attention.

"The neighbor?" she asked, her tone still calm, but her pen had started to move again.

"Yeah." I looked down at my hands. "I didn't know it was him at first. I was just...spiraling. Completely. The second the lights went out I was eight years old again, upside down, drowning in metal. And he was there. With me."

Becky nodded. "What did he do?"

"He didn't leave." My voice caught on the edge of the word, like it didn't know whether to tremble or flatten. "He stayed. Kept talking to me. Kept saying things like it was normal. Like I wasn't shaking like a live wire."

"Did you feel safe with him?"

"Yes," I said too fast. I paused. "Which is...rare."

"Why rare?"

"Because most people don't know what to do with me when I come apart. They either freeze or try to fix me like I'm a broken toy. But he didn't. He just...stayed."

Becky's gaze softened. "And that made you feel...?"

"Exposed," I admitted. "And warm. And furious. All at once."

I laughed, bitter. "I don't even know him. Not really. He's Thierry's brother. My brother-in-law. And I've barely looked him in the eye since moving in next door. But he knew exactly who I was. Of course he did. Men like him always know things they're not supposed to."

"Men like him?"

"Controlled. Dangerous. Collected. But charming enough that you forget all of that for half a second." I paused, then said quietly, "He called me *mon cœur*."

Becky smiled just slightly. "My heart."

I looked down at my lap. "It felt like a line. But also...not."

"Did it feel manipulative?"

"No," I whispered. "That's the problem."

Becky nodded once, slowly. "You said it made you feel exposed. Why do you think that is?"

"Because...I didn't want anyone to see me like that." I swallowed hard.

21

"Curled up on the elevator floor like a broken circuit. But he saw it. All of it. And instead of walking away—he wrapped his arms around me like I wasn't something to flinch from."

Becky was quiet a beat. "Did he make it worse?"

I shook my head. "He made it better. And now I don't know what to do with that."

"Why?"

"Because if he's kind once, I'll start hoping he stays kind."

"And is that so dangerous?"

"Yes," I said without hesitation. "Because people like me don't survive hope."

Becky sat back in her chair, tapping her pen once against the notebook. "Maybe you're not just surviving anymore. Maybe you're learning to be seen without burning."

I blinked again, slower this time.

"I don't even know if he saw me," I murmured. "Or if he saw someone fragile and decided to help. But in that moment—it felt like he saw the whole wreckage. And didn't flinch."

"I didn't know who he was," I blurted. "I just freaked out. Like—full spiral, ugly cry, the whole thing."

Becky raised an eyebrow. "In the elevator?"

I flopped onto the couch and groaned into my hands. "Yes. I'm so freaking embarrassed. Like...catastrophic embarrassment. Blackout-level."

She waited, the way she does.

"I thought I was alone, and then I realized I wasn't, and instead of holding it together like a semi-functioning adult, I basically collapsed in front of a stranger."

Becky tilted her head. "But you said you didn't know who he was?"

"I didn't," I said quickly. "Not at first. I mean...I know now. It was Matteo DuPont."

That got her attention. "Your neighbor?"

"Yeah." I let my head fall back against the couch. "Of course it was him. Hot, slightly smug, smells like expensive soap and danger. He's basically allergic to elevator panic and I gifted him mine for forty-five straight minutes."

Becky smiled softly. "And what did he do?"

"He...didn't freak out. He talked to me. Kept cracking these dry, ridiculous jokes like we were in a rom-com instead of my literal night-mare scenario."

I laughed, weakly. "He was nice. Like, *actually* nice. Not performative. Just...solid."

"And how did that make you feel?"

"Like I wanted to die more, honestly."

I threw a pillow at my face and groaned again. "He was cute and calm and I was curled into a human pretzel sobbing into his shirt."

Becky let the silence settle before gently asking, "Why does nice make you feel like that?"

"Because it's unfamiliar. And temporary."

I peeked over the pillow. "Nice is fine. But when nice comes with perfect bone structure and arms that feel like home and he calls you *mon cœur*, you start to unravel."

Becky paused. "He called you *mon cœur?*"

"Yeah. And that's when I mentally checked out and entered full existential crisis mode."

She gave me a small, knowing smile. "So...you felt seen."

"I felt ambushed by kindness. By someone I didn't know I wanted to be seen by."

She leaned in slightly. "And what happens if you let yourself want more?"

I blinked at the ceiling. "Then I have something to lose."

I sighed.

Of course that's what it was.

I sighed.

Of course that's what it was.

Being Malcolm Nash's daughter wasn't a legacy—it was a scar that never quite stopped itching. It opened doors I never asked to walk through and slammed others shut before I even reached for the handle. People either looked at me like I was royalty or a time bomb, depending on how well they knew him.

And the worst part? They weren't wrong.

There were pieces of him in me I couldn't deny—his precision, his hunger for control, that coiled instinct to strike first and regret later. I hated him. I owed him.

I survived because of him. I became someone people feared because I had to.

Unlike Talia.

Bright, untouchable, carrying their father's name like a shield rather than a weight. She had a way of making everything look effortless—the laughter, the love, even motherhood.

Sometimes I wondered if she knew how much that scared me. Because while she floated, I was sinking beneath the surface of all the expectations and ghosts that came with being Malcolm Nash's daughter. She had hope. I had survival.

And no matter how much I wanted to be proud of her, part of me was haunted by the fear that one day, she might understand the cracks I tried so hard to hide.

Because being Nash's daughter didn't come with a choice—it came with terms.

And every time someone brought up my name like it meant something, all I could think was—*You don't know what it cost.*

CHAPTER 7

Teo

SHE WAS TALIA'S SISTER.

Until that moment, I hadn't been sure. Until she confirmed it.

She was back.

I was on my way home.

She was there.

And she was terrified of tight spaces.

I took a breath—steady, measured—but inside, my mind was racing, trying to make sense of this fragile, trembling woman in my arms. This was my sister-in-law?

The one I'd kept at arm's length, the one Andrei warned me about?

I knew of her—everyone did. The girl with platinum hair and haunted eyes. But never like this. Not vulnerable.

Not raw and shaking under her jacket like she was a wounded bird too scared to fly. Afraid to take my hand.

Her fingers trembled against the fabric of my coat—expensive, sure, but nothing compared to the cost of what she carried beneath her skin.

The aftermath of her panic was a silent scream I could almost feel against my chest.

"Doucement."

I needed her to believe I was solid. That I wouldn't break her. Even if I wasn't sure I could hold myself together either.

"Close your eyes," I murmured, hoping she'd find some peace there—if only for a moment.

My body betrayed me, melting against her as if it had finally found something it had been aching for without even knowing.

Her scent mixed with the faint trace of gardenia on my skin, and I breathed it in, grounding myself in the moment, in the now.

The elevator hummed to life, but this time the sound didn't send her spiraling.

Not with her face tucked into the curve of my neck, her palm pressed lightly against my chest, steadying herself against my heartbeat.

"Almost there."

The same floor I called home.

The universe had a cruel sense of humor.

Trapping her and me in a steel box, alone but not alone. A stranger, a sister-in-law, a neighbor.

A puzzle I wasn't sure I wanted to solve.

I should let her go, put her down, insist she stand on her own.

But something inside me—the part I don't often show—wanted to hold her, protect her, be the solid ground she'd been starved for.

Her body remembered the darkness she'd escaped—the metal, the crushing weight, her mother's laughter like a poison in her ears. And now, it was learning to remember something else.

Strong arms. Quiet promises.

Soft words whispered in a language meant to soothe.

I wasn't used to tenderness. I didn't know how to give it without losing control.

But right now, I couldn't let go.

"Here we are," I said quietly as the elevator doors slid open. *"Mon petit cygne.* My little swan."

The teasing nickname, meant to make her smile earlier, hung heavy between us.

Teo DuPont. Billionaire. Playboy. Her brother-in-law.

CHAPTER 8

Tea

"WHAT DID YOU MEAN THERE WAS NOTHING?"

I swirled the whiskey in my glass, watching it catch the city lights flooding through my penthouse windows.

"I meant she was a ghost," Jace's voice came through clearly. "Natasha Nash existed on paper, but barely.

Father: Malcolm Nash, deceased. Mother: unknown. Every trace of her childhood—medical records, school records—it was like someone had gone through and systematically erased them."

I took a long drink, letting the burn match the one in my chest. "What about Nash Group?"

"That was the thing—she was set to inherit everything. The entire empire. But no one knew about her. It was like she was being groomed in the shadows."

Another secret. Another piece of Talia's world none of us had known about.

Just like Thierry.

My phone buzzed—Maxine. Again.

Probably with more threats about what she'd do to Andrei's company if he didn't cut ties with his bastard son.

The son she hadn't known about until last year. The son who was more my brother than she had ever been my mother.

The irony didn't escape me—here I was, digging into Natasha's secrets while drowning in my own family's lies.

"Keep digging," I told Jace. "I want everything."

I ended the call and walked to the window. Somewhere fifty floors below, New York continued its endless dance of lights and shadows. From up here, everyone looked like ghosts.

Including my reflection.

The woman who had shattered in my arms and then rebuilt herself with razor edges. The woman who looked at the world like it was full of shadows only she could see.

I recognized that look. I saw it in the mirror every morning.

We were all haunted by something. Andrei by his secrets. Maxine by her rage. Me by the emptiness no amount of success could fill.

And Natasha...what haunted the girl who could go from broken to lethal in the space of a heartbeat?

My phone buzzed again. Not Maxine this time—Jasmine. Or Jessica. One of the women who warmed my bed when the silence got too loud.

"Bonsoir," I answered, already reaching for my keys. "Give me twenty minutes."

I would go to her. Or to a club. Anywhere but here, where I could still feel the phantom weight of Natasha in my arms. Still smell magnolias in the air.

Some ghosts you could fuck away. Some you could drink into submission. And some...

Some took root in your chest and refused to leave.

I downed the rest of my whiskey and grabbed my jacket—not the one that still smelled like her. That one I had hung separately, like the trophy it wasn't supposed to be.

Another night. Another warm body. Another attempt to fill the void.

But as I stepped into the elevator—the same one where she had fallen apart in my arms—I knew it was pointless.

Because for forty minutes, I had felt something real.

And nothing in this world was more terrifying than that.

I had downed the rest of my whiskey, but it hadn't washed away the image of her—trembling, vulnerable, perfect.

There was a submission in her I hadn't seen before, something that couldn't be bought or negotiated.

Fuck.

I knew that look. I had spent years searching for it—in contract after contract, scene after scene—always chasing that rare balance between strength and surrender.

A slave who could meet me, challenge me, and then yield so beautifully it would make angels weep.

Natasha Nash—with her knife, her shadows, and her jagged edges—would have made an exquisite—

Her instincts were sharp—her anger a shield for a deeper need to surrender, a trust that had come before she even knew who I was.

In her fight and her surrender, in the way she responded to my voice, I saw something rare—an underlying strength that both challenged and called to me.

I drained the whiskey but couldn't shake the image of her—vulnerable, trembling, yet impossibly strong beneath it all.

Her trauma wasn't just surface deep; it pulsed beneath her skin, making her hyperaware, always poised between defense and surrender.

I'd seen that instinctive response to authority before—how she flinched yet obeyed, how her body shifted seamlessly from vulnerability to guarded strength.

It wasn't just submission; it was survival.

That delicate balance—the one I'd spent years chasing in contract after contract, scene after scene—wasn't something you learned.

It was innate. Real. It came from the core of a person's nature, not the mask they wore.

She wasn't playing at submission.

She *was* submission—raw, complex, and deeply intertwined with a need to control and be controlled.

The tells were everywhere: how she responded to my voice without hesitation, how her body surrendered during crisis, the flicker of trust before she even knew me, the fire that still burned when she fought back.

She fit against me like she belonged there—like her jagged edges were meant to be held.

I was both businessman and Dom, trained to read people in boardrooms and bedrooms. But with Natasha, it wasn't just skill—it was something visceral, immediate, undeniable.

She was exactly the kind of broken I wanted to hold together.

Andrei would have killed me.

Talia would have resurrected me just to kill me again. And Thierry... my brother, who'd already stirred enough family drama just by existing...

I picked up my keys, then set them down again. The club wouldn't help. Another submissive wouldn't help. Nothing could erase the way she'd felt in my arms—the way she'd trusted me before she even knew who I was.

The way she could be mine.

No. She was off limits. A complication I didn't need. A temptation I couldn't afford.

Even though every dominant instinct I had screamed to break down her door, to show her what real submission felt like, to piece her back together under my hands...

I pulled out my phone again. "Jace. I need everything you can find on her. Everything."

Knowledge was power. Maybe if I understood her, I could exorcise this ghost before it consumed me.

But as I stared at my reflection in the window—the predator lurking behind my eyes—I knew it was already too late.

And now every dominant cell in my body wanted her back.

CHAPTER 9

Natasha

I DIDN'T KNOW WHAT TO DO.

So I washed my hands—again and again—until the third time, when the skin on my fingers cracked and burned, raw and angry, and I realized I was scrubbing away something that wasn't dirt.

But what else could it be? The shadows had teeth now, claws scraping at the edges of my vision.

They slithered across the ceiling in slow motion, like ink spilled on glass, whispering in my mother's voice—taunting, mocking.

Sometimes they wore Malcolm's face. That cruel smirk so close I could feel his breath on my neck. I told myself it wasn't real.

My therapist said it wasn't real. But then what was this gnawing inside me, this relentless clawing at my thoughts that wouldn't let up?

You're broken.

You deserve this.

No one will save you.

My chest tightened. The air thinned. I tried to breathe but my lungs rebelled, crushing, tightening like a vise.

My fingers trembled, and the room spun slightly. Was it the meds?

Maybe. No, they twisted things inside me. Made the shadows bigger. Made the claws sharper.

"Natasha," Dr. Becky's voice came through my laptop, soft and steady, like a lifeline wrapped in velvet. "Have ye taken yer meds today, love?"

I stared at the line of orange bottles on my nightstand, each one a silent sentinel watching, waiting. "Yes," I whispered, voice barely a breath.

"That's a lie," she said gently, not angry—just sad. "The panic attacks won't stop if ye don't—"

I shook my head, tears burning my eyes. "They make it worse."

The shadows writhed. The claws scraped louder. The whispers grew, louder, closer, until I was drowning in the voices that said I was nothing, that I was lost forever.

I wanted to scream. I wanted to run. But my body was frozen—trapped in the black tide of my own mind.

And still, the hands kept washing, the skin burning, because it was the only thing I could control.

The shadows weren't just darkness—they were a wildfire creeping through my mind, an unrelenting blaze that devoured logic and reason, leaving nothing but scorched earth and smoldering ash in its wake.

They licked at the edges of my sanity, turning every thought into smoke and every memory into a charred ruin.

Fear clung to me like soot on skin—black, suffocating, impossible to scrub away.

"The shadows aren't real," Becky's voice floated through the haze, soft and steady, like a lighthouse beacon trying to cut through the storm. "The guilt ye carry—that's real. The trauma—that's real. But the shadows..."

I swallowed hard, the confession like shards of broken glass scraping my throat. "I killed him."

The words shattered the silence, echoing off the walls like a gunshot in an empty hall. "Malcolm. I killed Malcolm, and now he haunts me. He won't leave me alone."

"Ye saved Talia. And her wee babe."

Drew. My nephew. A fragile flame I barely dared approach, because the world outside had become a cavernous void, filled with echoes of pain and threats of darkness.

A knock at the door startled me—Sarah, my physical therapist, bearing the weight of hope in her smile and the promise of progress in her bag of tools.

She had been with me since the accident, since Mother had ensured my body would never be whole again.

"Bad week?" she asked gently, her hands already moving to stretch the scarred, stubborn muscles of my ankle.

"Aren't they all?" I murmured, my voice barely above the whisper of the wind outside my window.

The pain was sharp, tangible—a cruel gift that tethered me to the present.

Unlike the shadows that clawed at the fragile walls of my mind or the memories that threatened to drown me in their cold depths, the ache in my ankle was real, concrete, undeniable.

When Sarah left, I curled into the worn cushions of the couch, seeking refuge in the hauntingly familiar strains of *The Addams Family* theme song.

It was a fragile thread to the past—a secret ritual Talia and I shared, a pocket of light before the mask Malcolm wore cracked and shattered everything.

The music was a lullaby for the broken, a bittersweet reminder that even in darkness, there could be a twisted kind of family and belonging.

But as the final notes faded into silence, the shadows crept back, stretching their fingers across the walls of my mind, whispering that I was still alone in the dark.

"They're creepy and they're kooky..." I sang softly, chasing ghosts of a safer time.

Then the doorbell rang.

3:33 AM.

The bastard child of the witching hour.

But safety was a lie. A trick the universe played before it tore you apart.

The car flipped. Metal screamed. Mother laughed.

Malcolm's gun pointed at Talia's pregnant belly.

Blood. So much blood.

The shadows danced closer, wearing faces I couldn't forget. But then there was a new voice in my head, one that didn't belong with the monsters:

"Listen to my voice. You're safe. I've got you."

Teo. Always Teo now. His voice cut through the chaos like a blade of light.

I hated him for it. Hated how my body remembered the safety of his arms, how my mind played his words on repeat like a fragile lullaby. One elevator ride. One moment of weakness. And now he had infiltrated even my madness.

It didn't help that he looked so much like Thierry—the brother who held me through nightmares in Cape Verde, who never once looked at me like I was broken. But Teo wasn't Thierry. Teo was...

"Mon petit cygne."

The doorbell rang.

3:33 AM.

The witching hour's bastard child.

My body moved without permission, drawn by some force I didn't understand. The shadows followed, but they were quieter now, as if even they were curious about the man on the other side of my door.

I didn't remember crossing the room. Didn't remember punching in my security code. Didn't remember deciding to open the door.

But there I stood—a ghost in my own doorway, wearing week-old pajamas and carrying all my demons in my eyes.

Teo's smile faltered. Those alien-blue eyes widened just slightly as they took me in—all of me.

The tangled platinum hair. The dark circles under my eyes. The way I leaned against the doorframe because my ankle couldn't hold me up anymore.

He saw me. All of me. The shattered fragments and jagged edges, the rawness I tried so hard to hide—and everything tangled between.

No pretenses. No masks. Just the broken girl standing in the hallway, exposed and unguarded.

And for the first time in seven days, the shadows went quiet.

I hated him for that. More than anything.

Because when the darkness paused, I was forced to confront the aching ache beneath it—the fragile hope that maybe, just maybe, someone could see me without flinching.

I shouldn't answer.

The shadows were thicker tonight, wrapping tighter around my mind, and my grip on reality was slipping. But the security panel lit up again—his face, unmistakable.

Teo. Holding...flowers?

My body betrayed me before my mind could catch up.

I moved toward the door, muscles remembering the weight of safety in his arms, the steady rhythm of his heartbeat beneath my trembling fingers.

The shadows whispered—sharp and relentless—that I didn't deserve safety. Didn't deserve comfort.

Didn't deserve anything but the cold sting of pain.

Maybe they were right.

Still, I opened the door.

CHAPTER 10

Teo

THE MOMENT THE DOOR OPENED AND I GOT A FULL LOAD OF HER, I KNEW something was wrong. Deeply wrong.

And there I was—my idiot ass—showing up with daisies.

The woman standing before me was a mess, a beautiful, broken mess. Her clothes were barely clean, hanging on her like a second skin worn too long.

Her platinum hair was tangled, and her eyes—those haunted, ice-blue eyes—were rimmed with exhaustion and something darker, something raw.

Something fierce.

The sight stirred something primal inside me, something I usually kept locked away beneath layers of control and calculation.

The part of me that didn't just want to protect her, but to own that protection.

To be the wall she could lean on, the strength she could never admit she needed.

She leaned against the doorframe, her body trembling slightly, ankles weak beneath her.

But there was fire in her—a spark buried beneath the bruises, the shadows, the pain.

Standing there, I felt every dominant instinct I'd spent years training myself to ignore flicker to life.

The urge to take charge, to steady, to hold tight and never let go.

Because even broken, she was mine to protect.

She stood there in a blue baby doll nightgown, fragile and worn, like a porcelain doll someone had tried to piece back together—but the jagged edges still showed.

Dark circles shadowed those ice-blue eyes, heavy with exhaustion and secrets.

Her platinum hair fell in wild tangles around her face, as if the world had clawed at her and left her unraveling.

But it was her ankle that caught my attention—raw, scarred, a map of pain that had been deliberately etched into her skin.

Something in my chest tightened—a sharp twist of protectiveness and anger. No one had ever mentioned this to me. Not Andrei. Not anyone. What the hell had happened to her?

She swayed, just slightly, and I saw her slipping—slipping into that dark place behind those haunted eyes. That place where the ghosts whispered and hope felt like a distant memory.

So I did the only thing I could think of. I stepped forward and lifted her into my arms, pulling her close, holding her like she might shatter all over again if I let go.

There was something in her brokenness that called to me—called to the part of me that wanted to gather all those sharp edges and smooth them out, to claim her pieces and own them, to make her safe beneath my hands.

Dangerous thoughts, DuPont.

But as she melted against me, just like she had in that elevator, I knew I was already lost.

Because broken recognizes broken.

And whatever demons haunted Natasha Nash, they danced with mine like old friends.

Seven days.

Seven fucking days of watching her door, listening for any sign of movement, knowing she was unraveling behind that thin wall.

Sleep evaded me again that night, my mind looping the same relentless thoughts: her trembling in my arms, the knife arcing toward me, the way she surrendered before even knowing who I was.

The files Jace sent only dug the knife deeper. A car accident at eight years old. Multiple surgeries. Her mother's name redacted from every document—like some dark secret erased from the official record. The pieces painted a portrait I didn't want to see.

A portrait that matched the screams I'd heard through the wall at 2 AM.

The daisies had been a mistake. A moment of weakness grabbed at the 24-hour bodega downstairs. Something pure and innocent to counterbalance the darkness that clung to both of us.

I told myself I'd just leave them there. Walk away. Stop letting her infiltrate my every thought.

But then I heard it—her voice, that fragile, broken melody drifting through the wall.

"They're creepy and they're kooky..."

Putain.

Before I could stop myself, I was at her door. 3:33 AM. The witching hour's bastard child.

When she opened it, something inside me shattered and reassembled all at once. She looked like a ghost—sharp edges, dark circles, and that scarred ankle I couldn't stop fixating on.

My dominant instincts roared to life—fix, control, protect, possess.

But this wasn't about control.

This was about keeping the one thing I didn't want to lose.

"Mon cœur, you're going insane all alone," I murmured, lifting her fragile frame into my arms, holding her close like she was the only anchor left in this godforsaken storm.

"What the fuck—" she growled, voice rough and raw with panic.

"No, don't freak out. It's just me—"

"I know."

I held her tighter as her body trembled uncontrollably, shaking like a fragile leaf caught in a storm. Nightmares. PTSD. Hospitalizations.

Two simple words, soft and broken, but weighted with everything she'd tried to bury.

Like she'd been waiting—waiting for someone, anyone—to witness her unraveling without turning away.

I recognized that tone. Heard it echo in my own voice on the nights when the silence screamed too loudly in my head.

The daisies I'd brought were already forgotten, lying discarded on the floor as I carried her inside and kicked the door shut behind us.

This wasn't about dominance anymore.

It wasn't about family obligations, or the obsession I'd fought to suppress.

It was about two broken souls, stripped bare, recognizing the shadows that danced behind each other's eyes.

And maybe that was the most dangerous thing of all.

Ironically, I broke the silence. "Talia asked me to come check on you when she told me you lived here in my building."

She froze.

"She said she hasn't heard from you in days."

"You need to stop fighting me," I murmured into her hair as she twisted in my arms, trying—half-heartedly, I noted—to wriggle free. "Because you're not winning this one."

"If you don't get out—" she snapped, her voice a brittle edge of panic and exhaustion.

"I'd love to see you try," I said calmly, tightening my grip, not in force, but in reassurance. "Can you just...not freak out for two seconds? I'm running on three hours of sleep and bad decisions. Ironically, Talia asked me to check on you when she told me you lived in the building."

She stilled instantly.

"She said she hasn't heard from you in days."

A tremor ran through her. Not rage this time. Fear.

"You didn't tell her about the elevator."

"No." I settled back into her couch, keeping her in my arms like she was something precious I couldn't afford to drop. "That's between us."

She stopped struggling, but her muscles remained rigid against mine —tense, like she was bracing for impact.

The television flickered across the room, casting pale shadows across her living room walls.

The Addams Family played on mute. The irony wasn't lost on me. Trauma survivors clinging to morbid humor like it was oxygen. I got it. Hell, I *lived* it.

Her breathing began to steady—slow, shallow inhales giving way to deeper ones. My heartbeat synced to hers, a rhythm I hadn't realized I'd been searching for.

And then the unthinkable happened.

I fell asleep.

Wrapped around a woman I was never supposed to touch.

When I woke up, sunlight was just beginning to stain Manhattan gold.

The warmth of her was still tucked against me, her platinum hair spread across my chest like silver thread. She was curled into me, all sharp edges and soft vulnerability, and for one quiet moment, I let myself feel it.

The weight of her trust. The danger of it.

I should've stayed. Waited until she woke up. Said something that made this less complicated.

But I wasn't what she needed. Not really.

So I eased away—slow, careful, like I'd break her if I moved too fast— and slipped out the door before the sun fully rose.

Leaving behind daisies on the counter. And a part of me I didn't recognize anymore.

I hadn't planned on coming here.

Not really.

But I hadn't planned on losing sleep over her either.

And yet, here I was—wide awake at three in the damn morning, standing outside her door with a fistful of daisies and a head full of static.

I'd been restless for days. The elevator incident played on loop in my mind—her panic, the sound of her breath hitching, the way she'd tucked her face into my neck like I was a lifeline. I hadn't been able to let it go.

Jace had pulled the basics—her medical record was sealed, but enough breadcrumbs were left behind. Admissions. ER visits. That one arrest for "trespassing" that Andrei had buried. The more I saw, the more I understood.

She hadn't left her apartment in nearly four days. I knew because I watched the building's logs—don't ask why, I just did. At first it was curiosity. Then concern. Then something else. Something darker.

I told myself it was justifiable. Family. She was technically my sister-in-law. That gave me a sliver of moral ground to stand on, even if it wasn't solid. But I wasn't fooling myself.

Not completely.

The truth was, I couldn't get her out of my head. The way she responded to my voice in that elevator—instinctively, like her nervous system recognized mine. I'd seen women cry. I'd seen submission. I'd seen real trauma, the kind that doesn't heal with time or therapy. But I hadn't seen *that*.

And I hadn't expected it to affect me like *this*.

So yeah, maybe the daisies were a weak attempt at softening the edges.

An offering. Something bright and harmless to counteract everything else I was bringing to her door. My presence. My questions. My obsessions.

Because the truth was, I needed to *see* her.

Not just physically. I needed to know if she was okay. If she was eating. If she was still swimming in the dark, or if she'd found the surface again.

And yeah, maybe part of me needed her to see *me*. To recognize whatever passed between us wasn't some isolated moment in a broken elevator.

The part that scared me most?

It wasn't just concern.

It was need.

I needed to understand her.

I needed to *own* that memory.

I needed to know why my demons had gone quiet when she curled into my arms.

CHAPTER 11
Natasha

I WOKE UP TO EMPTINESS.

The kind I was used to—the kind that usually wrapped around me like a second skin, cold and familiar.

But something was different this time.

The air in the room didn't press in so hard.

The shadows that normally coiled in the corners like they owned the place were...still. Watchful.

Like they were waiting to see what I'd do now that he was gone.

Teo.

The name echoed through my head like a soft chime, intrusive in how easily it settled there.

His scent lingered on the couch. Sandalwood and something richer, darker. It clung to my skin, my clothes, the throw blanket someone—*he*— must've pulled over me.

I should have felt invaded. Violated, even.

But instead, the silence he left behind made me feel like I'd finally come up for air after years of drowning.

I sat up slowly, wincing as the ache in my ankle reminded me of everything I'd rather forget. And then I saw them.

The daisies.

Perched on the coffee table like they belonged here. Like something good could live in this space without being ruined.

They were still fresh, impossibly white against the grays of my living room. Simple. Sweet. So aggressively innocent I could hardly stand to look at them.

They were the kind of thing a man gives a woman when he doesn't know how to say, *"I see you."*

When he's trying to be gentle without admitting how much he wants to be. They were everything Teo DuPont wasn't.

And yet, he'd left them here. For me.

I touched one of the petals, soft between my fingers. It didn't wilt under my hand.

Everything leaves me eventually. My parents. My friends. The version of safety I clung to before I understood what it meant to lose it. No one ever stayed. No one ever really wanted to.

But last night...last night the demons didn't scream.

The ghosts didn't pull me under. The noise that lives in my chest—the constant hum of panic and grief and old rage—it went quiet.

He made it quiet.

And now?

Now I was terrified.

Because I could already feel the itch building in my skin.

The addiction.

To his voice.

To his steadiness.

To the way he didn't flinch when I broke.

To the way he touched me like I wasn't fragile, just rare.

I hated him for it.

And I hated myself more—for wanting it again.

For wanting *him*.

Fuck.

CHAPTER 12

Teo

"YOU...SLEEP...SLEPT...WITH THIS PERSON?"

Blue-eyes widened on the little bundle of fluff in his arms.

I never thought I'd see Lucas Devereaux become a father. Let alone one who watched what he said.

Our conversations used to be candid.

Now they had the open-ness of a can of tuna.

Lucas Devereaux was six-feet-two inches of pure Dad mode right now with his daughter Belle at five years old. Wheat-hair and blue eyes and a white-button down slightly wrinkled now from his daughter falling asleep—Lucas looked like the picture of the dad he hadn't had.

And one I didn't really think too hard about being until I met her.

In a green dress and her pink dinosaur toy she had her arms around him. Rubbing her eyes. Yawning.

Doing whatever it was a five-year old who apparently had the entire building enthralled did.

Uncle Teo was always at the rescue if she needed—but I was already an Uncle to an enormous baby Drew.

Lucas rubbed her chocolate cherry colored hair down to her elbows. She looked like a little princess.

The last time I'd visited him was a while ago. His office had changed to a bigger space. I had sold the old Roadsters location and moved into a bigger building as well.

And I remember the last time we met like this was years ago where we talked about his wife. Or rather the first time he met her.

Not now.

Now he was a father juggling babysitting his kid with meetings because he wanted to bring her to work.

"I have to put Belle down for her nap, but otherwise I have time to talk before Evie comes to lunch."

never went out to eat in public with people. It never ended well. Too many eyes. Too much noise. Too many expectations. I preferred control, privacy, and silence—things restaurants rarely offered.

"I like her."

"You like someone?"

"She doesn't want anything from me," I said quietly. "Not money. Not access. Not leverage."

He smirked lightly. "Let me put Belle down and we can talk. I was waiting for a while to find out what the fudge happened to you."

I smirked now watching him wondering if Natasha saw her nephew often.

But right about now, I was wondering if *Natasha* did.

Did she go out to eat? Or did the thought of crowded spaces, open air, and too many variables shut her down before she even tried?

Not that I was planning to take her. That wasn't what this was. I wasn't *inviting*. I was...curious.

Lucas mentioned Evie was coming by for lunch, and I was supposed to join them.

But Lucas was notoriously private, and Natasha?

She made private look public. She was the definition of closed off—locked down, emotionally encrypted.

Still, the idea stuck.

Would she go?

Could she?

Not because she felt obligated. But because she felt safe.

And would it be different if I was there?

I didn't like how easily that thought rooted itself.

The thought rooted itself quiet, like a bud and once it was there? It stayed because everyone around me had settled.

Everyone.

My older brother Andrei had married Talia a few years ago and they

45

had two sons. Lucas had a daughter. And my youngest brother Thierry had been in a relationship forever.

Forever.

My brothers who were like my best friends had all worked to be with their significant others. A fact that had terrified me.

And I couldn't stop thinking about *her* in that regard.

Not just in passing. Not just in the memory of her trembling in my arms in the elevator.

No. I thought about her *in private.*

I thought about her the way Lucas used to talk about Evie before they ever got together—like she lived under his skin and it drove him crazy. I thought about her late at night, when the penthouse was quiet, when the whiskey didn't burn as much as it should've.

And worse—I imagined her in love with someone else.

Someone like Lucas. Like Thierry. Someone capable and kind and steady.

The image sat wrong in my gut. *Didn't* sit, more like—*clawed.* Jealousy bloomed in me like a bruise under the skin. Slow. Dark. Deep.

It wasn't just envy. It wasn't just ego. It was a sensation. A *need* that scraped at the inside of my ribs.

I didn't want what they had.

I wanted what they couldn't even name.

Something *real.* As real as Drew toddling around the living room calling everyone "boo." As raw as Thierry's late-night study sessions and Avani's gentle, stubborn patience. Something *messy* in all the ways that felt good for the soul, even when it burned.

And right now, all I wanted was one platinum blonde who didn't even understand the kind of heart she had—how goddamn *golden* it was.

She didn't play games. Didn't flirt. Didn't ask for anything.

The women I knew wanted status. Money. Protection. Control. They always wanted something.

But *Natasha?*

She just wanted to be left alone.

And that made me want to get *closer.*

Not out of conquest. Not even out of curiosity anymore.

It was *need.*

Not the kind you fuck away or fix with a deal.

It was the kind that lingered. That changed you. That got under your skin until you forgot what it felt like to be untouched.

I had slept in the same bed as her—and I hadn't touched her.

That had never happened before. Ever.

And now, I didn't know what I wanted from her. Only that I wanted *more.*

She wasn't chaos. She wasn't calm. She was a contradiction I couldn't solve, a locked door I didn't want to break down but wanted to be *invited* through.

And fuck me—

That invitation might ruin me.

CHAPTER 13

I SENT HER THE DAISIES.

Every week, like clockwork. Simple. Anonymous.

My assistant probably thinks I'm insane—not that it's her business. But then again, managing a luxury car empire while juggling family politics does require a certain threshold of madness.

Speaking of which...

"Mr. DuPont?" A throat clears. "The projections for Q3?"

Right. Cars. Profit margins. Reality.

My phone buzzes.

Jace's weekly update on Natasha Nash.

Still listed as CEO-in-training at Nash Group.

Still absent from social pages.

Still ordering takeout at three in the morning.

Still haunting my thoughts like a song I can't stop humming.

I should stop.

Stop having her monitored.

Stop sending flowers.

Stop caring.

But every time I try, I remember her eyes—fractured light in a house of mirrors.

I remember the weight of her in my arms, the way she clung even as she tried to disappear.

I remember thinking: her demons recognize mine.

"The Singh merger—" someone starts.

"Is off the table." My voice is calm steel. "Family and business don't mix."

Hypocrite, something in me whispers. *Then why are you still watching her?*

Because she's different.

Because she's broken in all the places I know too well.

Because sometimes, late at night, I still hear her humming that ridiculous Addams Family theme song through the wall—and for just a moment, the silence doesn't win.

Six months of stabilizing Thierry.

Six months of crisis calls, PR disasters, and restructuring boards.

Six months of wondering if she's still unraveling.

Maybe it's time to find out.

I didn't expect her to trust me.

But I could offer mentorship. A lifeline, if nothing else.

And I did.

If she had a question, my line was always open.

And for a while, she used it.

Our messages stayed professional. Clean.

Text. Call. Clarification. Decision.

She was sharp—thoughtful in ways most interns weren't.

But eventually the calls dwindled. I got caught up in Thierry's storm with Talon and his former mentor.

And somewhere in all of that, I stopped noticing how often she reached out.

Until the texts disappeared altogether.

And I realized I missed them.

Worse, I realized I missed her.

CHAPTER 14

Natasha

"I'll just be ten minutes," Talia called from the shower. "You've got him?"

"Yeah." My voice came out flat—distant, even to me. "We're good."

Drew grabbed my finger with his chubby hand, and something in my chest cracked open. He was so pure. So innocent.

His eyes held nothing but trust as he looked up at me, like I was safety itself.

"Worthless little bitch."

Mother's voice cut through my mind like glass. "Can't even walk right."

I stared at Drew's perfect little ankles, his tiny feet kicking in the air. How could anyone…?

How could a mother look at something so helpless, so pure, and want to—The tears came without warning.

Metal screamed.

Glass shattered.

Blood ran down my leg as she stood there, texting.

"Maybe if you break enough, they'll fix you right this time."

The nursery spun. Memories crashed over me like waves—cold and merciless.

The hospital.

The surgeries.

Mother smiling sweetly as she told the doctors I wasn't following physical therapy.

Her hand on my shoulder, nails digging in, performing her best impression of a concerned parent.

"Such a difficult child. So clumsy. Always hurting herself."

But Drew...Drew was perfect.

Talia would never speak to him like that. The way I was spoken to. The way I talked down to and belittled.

Whole.

You'll never be anything in life.

Protected.

You'll never accomplish anything in life.

No one will ever want you. Not with that limp. Not with those scars.

His little hands reached for my face. I blinked, and in his eyes, I saw my reflection—no shadows, no demons.

Just...me.

The car flipped.

I screamed.

She laughed.

"Mama, please—"

"Don't call me that. You're nothing to me."

But Drew called Talia *Mama*, and she answered with love.

She kissed his forehead. Held him close.

Protected him.

The way a mother should.

The shadows pressed in, close and cruel, but Drew's laughter sliced through them like sunlight.

Like Teo's voice in the elevator.

Only purer.

Softer.

Innocent.

"Worthless," the echo hissed again.

But for the first time, I wasn't sure it belonged to me.

No.

"Broken."

No.

Teo's small hand found mine again, and the truth hit me hard.

I would die for this child. No hesitation. No question.

I'd kill for him, too, if it came to that. Because this—this quiet, steady kind of love—It's what I should've had.

What she stole from me. The tears came fast, and I couldn't stop them. But they didn't feel like weakness this time.

They felt like release. Like something old and heavy finally breaking loose.

Teo didn't seem scared. He didn't pull away.

He just kept his hand in mine and leaned into me like it was the most normal thing in the world.

He didn't care that I was a mess. Didn't care that I hadn't figured out how to be okay.

He just wanted comfort—and somehow, that made me feel like I had something to give. I held him close, blinking through the tears.

It wasn't panic. It wasn't shame.

It was grief, sure. But there was something else underneath it—something sharper. Rage.

At her. At what she took. At what she twisted and ruined.

I stared at the soft curve of Teo's cheek, the way his lashes fluttered as he started to drift off, and I knew without a doubt—

I would protect him with everything I had.

Even the broken parts.

Because he deserved better.

And maybe, just maybe, so did I.

$\sim$

"OH, TEO."

Talia's arms wrapped around me from behind, but I couldn't look away from Drew.

"What's wrong?" she asked gently.

"How?" My voice cracked. "How could she...?"

Talia didn't ask who *she* was. She didn't need to.

"I look at him," I whispered, "and I can't—I can't understand. He's so small. So perfect. I'd die before I let anyone hurt him."

Drew giggled then, that soft, belly-deep baby laugh that sounded like sunlight. He reached for my hair again—platinum strands wrapped around his chubby fingers like spun sugar.

And I let him.

Because something about his joy made it feel like my heart was cracking open in the best possible way.

"Some people," Talia said softly, "don't deserve to be mothers."

Mother's voice stirred in the back of my mind, bitter and sharp—but Drew's laughter drowned it out. It reminded me of Teo's voice in the elevator. But this? This was even softer. Brighter. Untouched by pain.

"He's huge," I murmured, trying to shift the conversation before I unraveled. "Are you sure he's only six months?"

Talia let out a teary laugh. "Andrei was a big baby too."

Drew grabbed my finger again—tight, trusting—and the feeling that washed over me wasn't panic. It wasn't fear. It was clarity.

I would kill for this child.

Not from rage.

Not from instinct.

But from love.

The kind that wraps itself around your ribs and makes you willing to burn the world down just to keep someone safe.

And for the first time in my life, I felt it—the ache of something I didn't know I wanted.

Not a child right this second.

But *a chance*.

A future where maybe I could be something more than the damage left behind.

Where I could love someone like this. Protect someone like this.

Where I could be a mother—and *not become her*.

The thought scared me. But it didn't feel impossible.

The shadows inside me went quiet, like even they knew better than to speak in a moment like this.

I moved like a ghost through the hallway, key in hand, already halfway to disappearing behind my door when I heard his.

Click. Open. Footsteps.

I froze.

"Oh, *mon cœur*," his voice called softly, almost amused. "Running again?"

I bolted.

But not fast enough.

An arm wrapped around my waist like iron, yanking me back against a body I knew too well. Solid. Warm. Unyielding.

"Not so fast," he murmured.

Fuck.

His chest pressed to my back, and I hated how my body remembered him. The sandalwood.

That darker, almost-spiced scent that had clung to my sheets for weeks after the elevator. The one that haunted my dreams even when I begged my mind for silence.

"Six months," he said, his breath warm against my hair. "And not even a thank you for the flowers?"

"Let me go."

"No." His voice dropped, low and certain. "I don't think I will."

CHAPTER 15

Tea

I carried her into her apartment like she weighed nothing—though everything about her presence felt heavy. Heavy with exhaustion. With chaos. With pain.

The contrast between her world and mine hit immediately. Where my space was sharp edges and order, hers was soft clutter and quiet mayhem. A place where the walls hadn't been touched in months, maybe longer. A place that screamed *I'm trying,* even as it whispered *I'm drowning.*

Orange prescription bottles lined the coffee table like forgotten soldiers. Some full. Some empty. A few sideways, as if she'd knocked them over and never bothered to pick them up.

She squirmed in my arms. "Put me down—'

"No." I walked us to the couch and sat, settling her across my lap like the delicate, stubborn porcelain doll she was. "I think we're done with you making decisions for a while."

Her spine stiffened immediately. "You can't just—"

"I can," I said calmly, smoothing my hand over her thigh. "And I will. Because letting you handle everything on your own? It's clearly not working, *mon cœur.*"

Her body tensed, but I caught the flicker of something else in her eyes. Shame. Fear. A small, aching kind of relief.

"You don't know anything about me."

I leaned in, voice low. "I know enough."

I nodded to the pills. "You haven't taken your medication consistently in weeks." I reached for her takeout bag near the sink. "You order food in the middle of the night because you forget to eat during the day." My eyes found hers again. "And I know you haven't shown up to physical therapy since the elevator."

She turned her face away. "Have you been stalking me?"

"Monitoring," I said, gripping her chin and gently turning her back to face me. "There's a difference."

She glared. "That's—"

"Insane? Controlling?" I murmured into her hair, breathing her in. "Welcome to my world, *mon coeur*. You're the one who stepped into it."

Her lips parted, but no words came out. Just shaky breath. The kind that came after holding everything together too long.

Her eyes blinked fast, lashes catching the light, and I could see how close she was to unraveling again.

"So I propose an agreement." My tone softened slightly. "You let me stay. Just for a while. You get in bed. I get in behind you. No talking. No arguments."

"And then what?" she asked, barely above a whisper.

I leaned in until our foreheads nearly touched. "Then I hold you until your shadows go quiet."

～

"I'VE SLEPT LIKE SHIT," I SAID, MY VOICE LOW, BRUSHING A PIECE OF HER hair off her shoulder. "So I'm going to propose an agreement."

Her body stiffened in my lap. Good. She was listening.

"Twenty-four seven." My fingers moved slowly, deliberately, drawing idle circles on her spine. "I already have the contract. Drafted. Reviewed. Annotated. It's been on my desk longer than I care to admit."

She didn't move, but her breath caught in her throat.

"You'll still run Nash Group," I continued. "But you'll do it without running yourself into the ground. I'll help you—manage, delegate, rebuild. You won't fail, because I won't let you."

I let that sit, just long enough to land.

"In return," I said softly, "you belong to me. Entirely. Every inch. Every hour. Every thought. Your body, your choices, your submission. All of it." My thumb brushed over her lower lip. "And not just physically."

She tensed under my hands—but she didn't pull away.

"You're going to open up to me emotionally," I said. "Just like you did physically. You're going to let me in. Every fear, every wound, every wall you've built—I want them all. I'll rebuild what I can. Burn down what I can't."

Her gaze flicked up, startled, but not in fear. In recognition.

"You're not a good man," she whispered. It wasn't an accusation. It was fact.

"No," I agreed. "I'm not. I'm possessive. Obsessive. The kind of man who sends daisies every week and has your schedule memorized down to your sleeping patterns."

A breathless sound caught in her throat. Almost a laugh. Almost a sob.

"But I'm also the man who sees you, Natasha. All of you. And I still want you. Especially the parts you're scared to show."

I dipped my head to hers. "You can think about it," I murmured. "But we both know your answer."

I stood, righting her gently. Something flickered behind her eyes— uncertainty, maybe. Or disbelief. Like no one had ever offered to carry her weight before without dropping her halfway.

"I'll send you the contract," I said.

And I did.

She signed it that night.

Because some contracts aren't just about dominance.

Some are about trust.

And some people—like her—don't need saving.

They just need someone willing to hold all their broken pieces without flinching.

~

KIERAN WAS SEARCHING FOR A FUCKING *PAINTING*, OF ALL THINGS.

Not a person. Not a weapon. Not a deal gone sideways or a financial leak in one of our offshore accounts.

A painting.

And the first thing I did?

I called Jace. Who called Monty. Because of course he did.

It wasn't that I didn't *want* to help Kieran. I did. I always did. He was my younger brother. The golden one.

The one who somehow turned every reckless impulse into poetry.

But this?

This was absurd. Even by our standards.

I stared at the forwarded file Jace had sent me—an inventory list with a missing item circled in red. Oil on canvas. Artist unknown.

Stolen decades ago. No record of sale. Supposed to be sentimental.

Kieran said it had belonged to our grandfather. That it meant something.

I wasn't sure if I believed that, or if this was just another distraction—another elegant excuse to avoid whatever was really bothering him.

Still, I called in favors. I reached out to the kind of contacts that don't answer phones unless the number glows red.

I burned a bridge or two, just because I could. Because even if I didn't understand *why*, I understood *who* was asking.

And that had always been enough.

But somewhere between the art gallery in Prague and the old forger in Marseille who owed me a debt, I realized something:

This wasn't about the painting. Not really.

It was about trying to reclaim something lost. Something *ours*. Something untouched by all the violence and inheritance and blood on our hands.

And maybe, deep down, I envied that.

Because I didn't chase lost things anymore.

I buried them.

And then I walked away.

To my new life.

CHAPTER 16
Natasha

His cologne was invading my space.

That dark, expensive scent that somehow managed to be both comforting and completely disorienting. Like sandalwood and sin. And I was having yet *another* breakdown.

Two days.

Two days of staring at a contract that outlined *everything*—from my sleeping schedule to what I was allowed to wear. Two days of my brain short-circuiting every time I read the word *"slave."*

Two days of rereading that moment:

"I can make you stop thinking," he'd said in that voice—the one made of dark velvet and terrible promises.

"H-how?"

His laugh had been maddeningly calm. "You won't approve."

"Try me."

"I want you to be my slave."

And I—goddess help me—hadn't run screaming. I'd listened.

Now I sat cross-legged on my bed in a hoodie that still smelled faintly of him, surrounded by tabs open on my laptop that I'd absolutely need to delete later. Terms like *"D/s dynamics," "consensual power exchange,"* and *"slave contract etiquette."*

Did being a sexual slave have business hours?

Did I get weekends off? Federal holidays?

Did OSHA regulate this sort of thing?

The contract sat on my nightstand like a sentient object—watching me. Judging me.

Teo had thought of everything, of course:

No more skipping meals
- *Mandatory therapy appointments*
- *Physical therapy three times a week*
- *A strict bedtime* (bedtime, *like I was five*)
- *No more 3 AM takeout binges*
- *Something called* aftercare *that I still couldn't think about without blushing*
- *An entire section on* submission protocols *that read like an erotic military manual*

The scariest part? It all made sense.

Not just in a logical way. In a *terrifyingly intimate* way.

Like he'd dissected my chaos, color-coded it, and reorganized it in French.

And somehow, I felt…seen.

When I showed up at his penthouse—because apparently, signing your soul away required a face-to-face meeting—I expected leather chairs, gold trim, and ominous mood lighting.

What I got was Teo answering the door in *pajama pants* and a worn hoodie.

Casual and Teo were not words that belonged in the same sentence. It was like seeing a lion in bunny slippers. My brain didn't compute.

"You're staring," he said, amused.

"You're…comfortable," I muttered, eyeing his bare feet like they were some kind of trap.

He stepped aside to let me in. "I figured if I showed up looking like a contract negotiation, you'd bolt."

Touché.

His place was warm. Lived in. Less intimidating than I remembered. There were fresh tulips on the counter—*my* favorite, because of course he knew that—and a tray with two steaming mugs of tea.

"You made tea?" I blinked.

"Chamomile," he said. "I also have scotch, if the idea of paperwork overwhelms you."

"Oh, I'm already overwhelmed. But thanks."

I took the tea anyway.

Because despite all the protocols and pages of rules...

Despite the word *slave* sitting on my nightstand like a loaded weapon...

This didn't feel like a power play.

It felt like an anchor.

And I didn't know whether to run or lean into it.

But for now, I drank the tea.

And didn't bolt.

His smile spread wide when he saw me. "Mon coeur."

I clutched my phone, still open to "BDSM for Beginners" like it was a shield. "I have questions."

"I assumed you would." He looked far too amused. "Starting with business hours?"

I flushed. "How did you—"

"Because you're adorable." He pulled me inside. "And because you've never done this before."

"That obvious?"

"Did you actually read the entire contract?" He settled on his couch, pulling me down next to him.

"Three times. I made notes." I pulled out my phone, opening my documents. "Page four, paragraph three—what exactly does 'complete surrender' entail? And why is there a whole section about bubble baths?"

His laugh was rich and dark. "Only you would annotate a slave contract."

"I'm thorough."

"So I see." He plucked my phone from my hands. "Did you get to the part about orgasm control yet?"

I choked on air. "The what?"

"Page twelve." His grin was positively wicked. "Though maybe we should start with the basics. Like how you're supposed to be kneeling right now."

"I thought that was just a suggestion—"

"Mon coeur," his voice dropped lower, "nothing in that contract is a suggestion."

Oh.

Oh.

"So..." I twisted my fingers together. "No employee handbook?"

He caught my hands, stilling them. "I'll be your handbook. Your guide. Your everything." His thumb traced my pulse. "Starting with teaching you how to breathe properly."

"I know how to breathe."

"Do you?" He pulled me down into his lap, his hands settling firm but gentle on my waist. "Because right now, you're about two seconds from full-on hyperventilating."

I swallowed hard, voice trembling. "This is all very new. Usually when I sign contracts, it's about art acquisitions or office leases—not...whatever the hell was on page twelve."

He chuckled low in my ear, breath warm and intoxicating. "Trust me," he whispered, "this will be a masterpiece."

The weight of those words pressed against my skin like the heat of his body beneath me.

I was going to die.

Right here.

In his doorway.

Wearing the outfit his contract specified.

Clutching my phone like it was a lifeline.

At least I'd die well-dressed.

His fingers traced light circles along my spine. "Look at me," he said, voice firm but tender.

I lifted my eyes, meeting his intense blue gaze.

No judgment.

No pressure.

Just him.

"Whatever happens," he said. "We do this *together*. One breath at a time."

And somehow, even with the contract burning a hole in my pocket and my heart racing like a runaway train...

That felt like the safest place on earth.

I wasn't expecting the conditions of being a sexual slave to include...vegetables.

Or hydration reminders. Or a mandatory bedtime.

Or a goddamn salad with every meal.

But here we were.

Apparently being someone's possession meant three chef-prepared meals a day, balanced macros, no more cereal, and shockingly good roasted carrots with honey glaze that I hated myself for enjoying. I had a private chef. A *private chef*, who showed up like clockwork and somehow made "healing food" sound sexy.

"You're not eating enough protein," he said once. I blinked at the lamb tagine in front of me. "Eat."

That was it. Just—*eat*. No room for argument. Not when he stared me down with those eyes like Arctic storms and French authority. So I did. And I hated how good it felt.

Also? There were slippers.

Silk pajamas replaced my ratty oversized shirts. My favorite hoodie vanished. Cashmere showed up. Fuzzy socks with anti-slip bottoms. Candles that smelled like bergamot and sandalwood. And, worst of all, a mattress topper so soft it made my childhood bed feel like a slab of concrete.

He was controlling everything in my life, down to the thread count.

And I hated it.

Except I didn't. Not really.

The scary part was how much of it made sense.

There was no sex. Not in a month. Not even a suggestive look. He didn't touch me when I was vulnerable. He didn't coax me into anything. Didn't so much as glance at me sideways when I walked around in one of the silk sets he insisted I wear to bed.

Instead, I got...*structure*.

And massages.

Therapeutic ones. For my feet, of all things.

A trauma-informed specialist who helped me work through the scar tissue on my ankles and knees, who never asked questions when I cried. Another *gift* from Teo.

Just like the pills he made sure I took on time, the physical therapy appointments he personally approved, the blackout curtains he had installed in my apartment without asking.

This wasn't dominance. This was madness.

Who *does* this?

Who watches a girl spiral and says, *let me rebuild your nervous system from the ground up?*

It had to be guilt. Or pity.

Did he feel sorry for me?

Poor broken Natasha Nash, the family liability. The girl with the limp and the thousand-yard stare. The ghost of a dynasty no one wanted to admit still had a name.

The daughter who killed her father.

The girl with nightmares that woke the neighbors.

Everyone always looked at me like that. Like something tragic. Something *almost* worth saving—if you didn't mind getting your hands dirty.

Mother made sure of it.

"She's so sensitive. So delicate. Look how clumsy she is. Look how difficult. We try so hard with her..."

Always with that tired sigh, that twist of her lips, like she was the one who deserved sympathy for having to raise me.

Like I was some cursed pet she couldn't return.

Teo didn't look at me that way.

That was what made this worse.

He didn't try to fix me with words or pity or therapy brochures. He just showed up—like some feral French caretaker—with pudding and precision, and the kind of terrifying patience that made me want to scream.

I was a problem.

And he treated me like a priority.

I didn't know how to hold that. Didn't know how to accept kindness that wasn't performative. Didn't know how to trust someone who seemed to want *nothing* from me in return.

No sex.

No praise.

No tears.

Just...healing.

The kind that felt like a punishment because it was so foreign.

And every day I followed the stupid schedule he built for me—PT, therapy, meals, rest—I felt more like a person.

And that scared me more than any collar.

Because if I became someone whole...what excuse would I have left to hide behind?

Malcolm was worse. Playing the doting father in public while plotting to kill his own daughter behind closed doors. At least Mother never pretended to love me.

And now Teo...

He was going to check in tonight, and part of me—the part that still remembered throwing a knife at his face—wanted to push him. Test my boundaries.

Because this had to be another trick. Another game. Another person pretending to care while collecting all my broken pieces to use against me later.

The way he touched me...like I was something precious. Something worth saving.

Lies.

I didn't want to feel...

Like I felt with Drew.

Not with Teo.

I didn't want that pure, clean feeling. That moment when the shadows retreated and everything made sense. Because feeling that with my nephew was one thing. He was innocent. Pure.

Untainted by the darkness that followed our family like a curse.

But feeling it with him?

That was dangerous.

Because Teo DuPont wasn't innocent. Wasn't pure. He was darkness wrapped in expensive suits and French endearments.

A predator playing at being a protector.

Just like Malcolm played at being a father.

Just like Mother played at being concerned.

Just like everyone who claimed to want to help me.

So why did his voice chase away my demons?

Why did his touch make the shadows retreat?

Why did part of me want to believe this was real?

"Such a difficult child," Mother's voice whispered. "No one will ever really want you."

She had to be right. Because the alternative—that Teo actually meant all of this, that he saw my broken pieces and wanted them anyway—that was more terrifying than any shadow that haunted me.

Wasn't it? So maybe if I pushed hard enough, he'd show his true colors. Prove he was just like everyone else who claimed to care.

Prove that this whole thing wasn't what it seemed.

Because if it was real—if he actually meant all of this...

I stared at my fourth pudding cup, wondering when eating dessert became an act of rebellion.

Fuck it.

Time to see what happened when the slave misbehaved.

CHAPTER 17

Tea

DID I KNOW MY SLAVE WAS UP TO NO GOOD?

No.

But the evidence was damning. Five empty pudding cups lined up like a sugar-coated confession. A sixth halfway done, spoon dangling from her fingers as she stared at the TV with the kind of focus that only comes when you're pretending not to notice me.

And then there was the shirt. Ratty. Oversized. Not one of the silk ones I'd replaced it with. No slippers. Bare feet on hardwood. Probably cold.

She was testing me.

And she knew exactly what she was doing.

I took a slow breath, counting in my head—not to calm myself, but to list the ways I was going to torment her. Lovingly. Precisely. Thoroughly.

She was playing a dangerous game with me.

The one I invented.

I'd been waiting for this moment. Watching it unfold day by day in those glacial blue eyes of hers, that stubborn chin, the way she bristled every time I showed her care.

Every time I sent the chef.

Every time I rescheduled her physical therapy when she "forgot."

Every time I reminded her to take her medication like clockwork.

She hated it. Hated me.

No—correction.

She hated what I represented: control without cruelty. Authority without violence. Attention that didn't come with strings or punishment.

She was terrified of the gentleness. Because it didn't make sense in her world.

Because it meant I *might* care.

Like a wounded animal, she kept testing the hand that fed her—waiting for it to strike.

Mon petit cygne. My little swan, all puffed-up feathers and bared teeth. Desperate to prove I was just like the others. That I would snap. That I would hurt her the moment she stepped out of line.

And I could. I *should*, technically—according to the contract she signed, the rules she agreed to, the protocols she'd read three times and still asked if "aftercare" required an NDA.

But punishment wasn't what she needed.

Not yet.

She needed to understand that some cages were built to protect, not imprison. That some masters didn't destroy.

She wanted me to be cruel.

But I would be much, much worse.

I would be *kind*.

"Did you eat any real food today, mon cœur?"

"No," she said, not looking at me. Her tone clipped. Defiant. Like a kitten trying to roar.

I bit back a grin.

"I heard you told your PT not to come today."

"I didn't tell her anything," she huffed. "I just...canceled."

She was curled on the couch, legs crossed, foot twitching. That pert little ass wriggling in irritation—or was it invitation?

I took a step closer. Watched the shift in her posture. The tiny tremor in her hands. The way her breath hitched ever so slightly.

Not fear.

Anticipation.

She was waiting for the snap. The demand. The discipline.

Instead, I crouched in front of her, slow and deliberate, until we were eye-level.

"Is your foot cold?" I asked gently.

Her eyes narrowed. Suspicious. Cautious. "What?"

I reached for her ankle. She flinched but didn't pull away. "Cold," I murmured, brushing my thumb over her skin. "No slippers again."

"You threw my old ones out."

"I gave you better ones." I tucked a throw blanket over her feet and leaned in, just enough to feel her breath falter again. "Do you know why?"

She shook her head, stubbornly silent.

"Because I don't like watching you suffer when it's unnecessary." My voice was quiet now. Deadly calm. "Because I notice the details. Because you are mine, and I take care of what's mine."

Her chin trembled before she caught it.

"You don't have to."

"Yes," I said, brushing a strand of platinum hair behind her ear, "I do."

She blinked, startled.

I didn't press further. Not tonight.

Instead, I stood and headed to the kitchen, retrieving the balanced dinner she hadn't touched. I brought it back and placed it beside her pudding cup collection with the calm of a man used to resistance.

Then I sat beside her, close enough for warmth, far enough to give her the illusion of space.

She stared at the meal like it might bite her.

I said nothing.

Just waited.

Because this wasn't a game I intended to win by force.

This was seduction by patience.

And one day, when she finally surrendered—*truly* surrendered—it wouldn't be because I broke her.

It would be because I built her back stronger.

And she knew it.

She wasn't good at this.

Not really.

I was so much better.

I'd spent years mastering control, studying body language, decoding silences like other men read spreadsheets.

But she—she was still new to this game.

Still trying to understand the rules while pretending she didn't care they existed.

I sat down beside her, not touching her, just close enough that my presence sank under her skin.

69

Her little toes—painted a defiant shade of electric blue—stopped wiggling the second I did.

The rest of her body followed, frozen in place like prey sensing a predator nearby. Not fear exactly. Not anymore. But wariness. Awareness.

Bristling with a tension I could practically taste.

Oh, mon petit cygne.

You have no idea what game you're playing. But I do.

"You seem tense," I said softly, letting the gentleness coat every word like honey.

Not the commanding Teo. Not the one she could rail against. The one who drives her mad with quiet control.

"Something on your mind?"

She didn't answer. Just reached for another pudding cup like it was a grenade. Her fifth? Sixth? I'd stopped counting.

Each one a sugary declaration of war. Each one another line crossed in the contract she'd pretended not to care about.

"Nothing," she said finally, her voice wrapped in faux nonchalance.

She peeled the lid back with practiced indifference. Like this didn't matter. Like I didn't matter.

But her fingers tightened slightly on the cup.

A tell.

I let my arm stretch along the back of the couch, not touching her, but close enough to make her spine straighten. She hated that.

The not-quite-contact. The anticipation.

She didn't know what to do with it.

"No?" I asked, tilting my head just slightly. "Then you won't mind explaining the pudding cups."

She didn't answer. Didn't flinch.

But I could see it in her eyes.

The debate.

Back down—or push.

Always push, Natasha.

Good.

Push me.

I leaned in, brushing a loose strand of hair behind her ear with maddening care. She stilled completely, like she was holding her breath. Like one wrong move and she'd shatter.

I looked down just as her hand tightened again.

Then she dropped the pudding cup.

Deliberate.

Calculated.

The wet splat hit the floor between us like a challenge tossed at my feet.

Her eyes met mine—cold and daring, but behind it, something else. Something brittle. A plea she didn't want me to hear.

I smiled.

Slow.

Dark.

Unforgiving.

"Oh, *mon cœur*..." My voice dropped into a velvet growl. "You're going to wish you hadn't done that."

She blinked.

I saw it then—the flicker of something sharp and vulnerable behind her walls.

Fear? No.

Hope.

Hope that I *wouldn't* give up on her. That I'd stay. That I'd play the game all the way through.

So I stood.

Not fast.

Deliberate.

I didn't raise my voice. Didn't snarl or scold or point at the mess like some disciplinarian with a rulebook.

I simply stepped in front of her, took her chin gently between my fingers, and made her look at me.

"You want to see what happens when you act out?" I whispered. "Then I'll show you."

But not in the way she expected.

Not punishment.

Not cruelty.

She expected a storm. But what I gave her was silence.

I walked away—to the kitchen. Cleaned the mess. Returned with a fresh plate of real food. Balanced. Warm.

I placed it in front of her and sat again, this time even closer.

"You're not in trouble, Natasha," I said, voice low. "You're in pain."

And I could feel her unraveling. Slowly. Quietly.

She didn't cry.

But her jaw clenched like she was holding back a scream.

"You're not broken," I continued. "You're scared. And you're testing me to see if I'll disappear like everyone else."

I leaned in until my lips nearly brushed her ear.

"I won't."

Then I kissed her temple—just once—and stood again.

"Eat."

She didn't move.

But she didn't look away, either.

And when I reached the door, I heard the soft clink of a fork against the plate.

Good girl.

The game had begun.

And now, I was playing for keeps.

CHAPTER 13

Natasha

"PUT ME DOWN!" I SNAPPED, BUT MY VOICE BETRAYED ME—THIN, SHAKING, uncertain. "Teo—"

"Non." His tone was final, effortless. Like gravity. "You wanted my attention, mon petit cygne. Now you have it."

He didn't even glance down as he carried me out of my apartment and into his. The door swung shut behind us with a soft, controlled click that still made me flinch. Not because of the sound—but because of what it meant.

I'd never been in his space before. Where mine was clutter and ghosts —Mother's whispers buried in every corner, Malcolm's face etched into the walls—his was pure intention.

Dark leather. Polished wood. No chaos. No past. No compromise. Just quiet, immaculate dominance.

Even the shadows in my head seemed to hesitate. As if unsure whether they were allowed in here.

Traitors.

"I believe we need to discuss proper behavior," he said, walking deeper into the room like he hadn't just hijacked my body and mind both.

"I didn't—"

"Six pudding cups." His voice dropped to a darker octave, the kind of sound that curled around your spine and took root. "No real food. No physical therapy. And that shirt…"

I glanced down at the worn tee I hadn't realized I was still wearing—

the one that clung to me like a second skin, soft with years and memory. I wasn't in the silk pajamas he'd given me. The ones that felt too delicate. Too clean.

"It's comfortable," I said defensively, even as heat crept up my neck.

"It's going in the trash." He didn't stop moving.

We passed a glass wall overlooking Manhattan, and in our reflection, I saw it—me, small and disheveled, curled against his chest like one of Mother's porcelain dolls.

The kind she kept on high shelves. The kind she smashed when they disobeyed.

And him? He didn't look like any man I'd ever trusted. He looked like power in a tailored suit. Like sin wrapped in patience.

Like the only person who'd ever scared the shadows into silence.

"You can't just—"

"I can," he said simply. "And I will. Because you, mon coeur, seem to have forgotten who's in charge."

My heart thundered in my chest. I'd wanted this, hadn't I? Pushed and tested and provoked him just to prove he'd break like the others. That he'd hurt me or walk away.

But he didn't break.

He held me tighter.

And somewhere deep inside me, something uncoiled—something dark and low and aching. Something that didn't want to run. Something that wanted to kneel.

"I don't like being controlled," I whispered, but it sounded like a lie even to me.

Like all the lies Mother used to mutter after slapping me across the face. Like all the lies Malcolm told while pointing a gun at Talia's belly.

Teo laughed. Not cruelly. Not kindly either. It was a sound full of dark understanding, of sharp edges smoothed by experience.

"No," he murmured near my ear, "you just don't like admitting you need it."

He turned down the hall, and I knew before he opened the door where we were going. The bedroom. His.

My stomach tightened.

We passed more glass, more order, more curated calm. There was no mess here. No chaos he didn't allow.

I could feel myself shrinking inside his arms, curling into something small and soft and breakable.

Not because I was afraid.

Because I wanted to be.

We stopped at the door. I felt the weight of his gaze even before he spoke.

"Cold?" he asked, voice almost mocking. "That's what happens when you don't wear your slippers."

"I'm not cold, I'm—"

"Nervous?" He said it like a promise. Like a reward. "Good. You should be."

Because this wasn't pudding on the floor. This wasn't throwing knives or snarling insults. This wasn't my domain.

This was his.

And unlike Mother's punishments or Malcolm's rules, his control didn't feel like destruction.

It felt like devotion.

And the worst part—the part that made my skin prickle and my thighs clench—was that I didn't want to run.

I wanted to see what happened if I stayed.

What have I done?

He tossed me onto his bed—Egyptian cotton sheets that probably cost more than my therapy bills—and I scrambled like a wounded bird, until he caught my leg. The quick snap of something made my breath catch.

"Teo—" His name came out like a prayer, like a plea, like all the words I'd never been allowed to say.

He made a tsk sound with his teeth, the kind that should have reminded me of Mother's disappointment but instead sent heat pooling low in my belly.

"Yes?"

"Teo, let me go—"

"No."

"Teo"

He moved with predatory grace, securing my other leg with the same silent authority that had undone me from the start.

The soft straps—black silk against my bare skin—hugged just above the tender line of my scar, avoiding it entirely.

That small act of mercy, that moment of quiet awareness, shattered something inside me that had calcified long ago.

Not all monsters, it seemed, came to take. Some came to pay attention.

The room was hushed but not silent—the delicate sounds of him moving with intention. A drawer sliding open. The low clink of metal on wood. The rustle of fabric.

My pulse stuttered, picking up speed, but not from fear. It was something else entirely—something primal, heavy with anticipation. Not the kind of dread that came from waiting to be punished, but the terrible beauty of being seen, prepared, chosen.

My ratty t-shirt clung to me like a shield, but it was useless now. It had ridden up, exposing the swell of my hips, the softness of my thighs, the curve of vulnerability I never let anyone see.

And still, he said nothing. Just tucked a pillow beneath me—under my hips, lifting me for him—not in a way that made me feel used, but in a way that made me feel...treasured. Positioned. Revered.

I swallowed hard, breath catching as the mattress dipped beside me.

The shadows in the corners of the room were quieter than usual. Even they seemed unsure what to make of this. For years they had danced to the sound of glass breaking and screams that never echoed back. Now they waited, silent, as if bearing witness to something sacred.

I wanted to speak. To fill the room with something other than my trembling. But words failed me, as they always did when it mattered most.

He ran a hand down my spine—slow, firm, grounding. His palm was warm, steady, sure. And then he bent down, his lips brushing my shoulder in a kiss so soft it broke me open from the inside out.

"You're not broken," he murmured against my skin, like he could feel the battle raging beneath it. "You've been waiting for someone to treat you like you're whole."

I felt the tears before I knew I was crying. Not because I was scared. But because part of me still didn't believe anyone could touch the ruins of my body and not turn away.

He didn't flinch.

Instead, he pressed his mouth to the curve of my back and whispered. "Let me worship what they tried to destroy."

My hands clenched into the sheets. Not from resistance, but from surrender.

For the first time in years, I didn't feel like prey.

～

"TEO?"

My voice emerged small and fragile, like the child I'd been, begging Mother to stop.

But this wasn't pain I feared now. It was pleasure.

"What are you—"

"Shhh."

More sounds in the darkness.

More movement.

The soft pad of his feet on hardwood like a predator circling.

"You wanted my attention, mon coeur. Now you're going to learn what that really means."

I tested the restraints, something primal stirring in my blood.

They held firm but didn't bite—unlike the metal that had crushed my ankle, unlike Mother's nails in my skin.

These bonds promised something different. Like everything else about him—controlled. Precise. A cage built to protect rather than imprison.

"Grip the headboard tighter, mon coeur," he murmured, his voice dark velvet against my nerves.

Cool air kissed places I'd never let anyone see, and the shadows retreated to the corners, as if they too wanted to watch what would happen next. My body trembled with anticipation and fear—not of him, but of how much I wanted this.

Oh God. Oh God. I've never done this. Never let anyone this close to all my broken pieces.

The bed dipped between my legs, and then—his lips on my spine, a trail of fire that chased away my mother's ghost. I froze, caught between running and surrendering.

Those kisses traveled lower, mapping territory no one had ever claimed. Each touch erased another scar, another memory, another whispered taunt from my past.

When his tongue found places I'd never dreamed of being touched, my world shattered and reformed.

"Teo." His name escaped like a prayer, like salvation.

"I'm going to take all of you, mon coeur. Not a single inch of your body is yours. It's mine." His words promised possession, but not the kind that broke. The kind that pieced back together. And then his tongue claimed me completely, and I dissolved.

I died. Or maybe I was finally born.

My fingers gripped the headboard until my knuckles went white, trying to anchor myself to reality as pleasure crashed through me in waves.

His cologne filled my lungs as I bit the sheets, desperate to stay quiet, to stay in control, to keep some part of myself.

But he wouldn't allow that.

He groaned, hands spreading me wider, demanding surrender.

This man wasn't just a demon—he was my demon, come to devour all my darkness and replace it with his own.

Heat and sensation consumed me, building toward something I'd never felt before. This wasn't how I'd imagined my first time, but now? Now I craved it. Craved him. Craved this exquisite surrender.

"Teo." His name became a mantra as he feasted on me like a starving man.

∼

His face fell when he pulled out and saw the blood.

My whimper of pain filled the space between us, raw and involuntary.

Teo froze.

I didn't breathe.

His gaze shot to mine, and when he saw the truth in my eyes—saw the shame, the ache, the silent confession—he swore under his breath, dragging a trembling hand down his face.

"Why didn't you tell me?"

But I couldn't answer. My throat had closed up, too full of tears and humiliation and confusion. Words failed me.

Teo didn't give me time to find them.

He was back between my legs in a blink, his body above mine, his expression torn between anger, guilt, and something deeper—something terrifying in its tenderness.

I felt the head of him again, pressing gently at my entrance, and this time...it didn't hurt.

He moved slowly, inch by inch, sinking into me with the kind of care that made my chest split open. His breath stuttered. Mine hitched. We both groaned.

Tears slid silently down my cheeks.

Teo kissed them as they fell—along my jaw, my temple, down my neck—like he could make them disappear one by one.

My body trembled beneath him, but he didn't rush. He didn't demand. He moved like he was trying to rebuild something he'd broken.

"I know," he whispered, voice dark velvet in my ear. "Spread your legs wider for me...there you go. Good girl. Now *breathe*. Exhale."

I obeyed.

And something inside me loosened.

"See what obeying gets you?" he murmured, voice thick with heat. "You let me in. You listen. And now look at you..." He thrust deeper, slower. Measured. *Controlling.*

"You're going to be such a good girl for me from now on, aren't you?"

I nodded, wordless, helpless.

He rewarded me with more. More of him. More of the pressure that built and built until it felt like my whole world was centered where he touched me.

"There you go," he whispered again. "So mindless for me when you're being fucked."

My tears wouldn't stop.

Not from pain.

From release.

From fear.

From surrender.

"I know," he murmured, his voice a drug. "I can feel it. You're so close—right fucking there, aren't you?"

I was. Every muscle in my body was locked. The pleasure was unbearable. My body didn't know how to hold it.

"Teo," I gasped, voice cracking. "I've never—"

"I know." His voice turned fierce, possessive. "Let me have it. It belongs to me. Give it to me, *mon cœur.*"

I shattered.

It wasn't gentle.

It was devastating. A rush of heat and sobs and pure, uncontrolled ecstasy. I bit down on his shoulder, crying out, the sound escaping my lips like a scream too long buried. My entire body arched into him, trembling and raw, as he drove so deep inside me I couldn't tell where I ended and he began.

Teo groaned, pushing harder, shuddering as he came with me, wrapped around me, *inside* me, like he needed to fuse us together to make it real.

And then everything went still.

His lips found the pulse in my throat, gentle again, reverent. His hands stroked my sides, anchoring me through the aftershocks.

That's when I snapped.

The first sob escaped without warning—deep, cracked, torn from somewhere I didn't know existed.

Then another.

And another.

Each one more painful than the last.

Not from him.

But from everything that had come before him.

All the years of silence. All the ways I'd kept myself locked away, untouched, unloved, unworthy.

I cried like I was bleeding out.

And Teo stayed.

He held me tighter.

He whispered things I couldn't process.

And he didn't move.

Not an inch.

Because he knew I didn't need anything else right now.

Just to be held.

Just to be *his.*

IT WASN'T UNTIL HE STOPPED—HIS HIPS STILLED, HIS LIPS BRUSHING GENTLY over the frantic beat at my throat—that I shattered.

The first sob that tore from me wasn't quiet. It was jagged, primal, ripped from somewhere deep and hollow inside me. A place I'd locked up years ago and buried under silence.

And the next sob hurt worse.

Because it wasn't from pain, not really.

It was from everything that had come before this—every moment I'd

80

believed I wasn't worth holding, every memory of being punished for needing too much, every time I was told love had to be earned through obedience or silence or survival.

Teo didn't move.

He just held me tighter.

One arm locked around my waist, the other stroking through my hair with deliberate gentleness that undid me even more. The way his body curled around mine—protective, possessive, patient—made my chest ache.

"There it is," he whispered. "Let it out, mon cœur."

I couldn't stop. I didn't want to.

I buried my face into his neck, letting every broken part of me rise to the surface. My tears soaked his skin.

My hands clawed weakly at his back, searching for something to hold onto—something real.

And Teo didn't flinch. Didn't pull away.

He kissed my temple, again and again. "I've got you."

I didn't know how long I cried. Minutes? Hours? A lifetime?

But at some point, I realized something terrifying and beautiful all at once: I was safe. With him. In this bed. In this moment.

And that realization unraveled me all over again.

Later, when I was quieter—wrecked, but calm—he tilted my face up, brushing his thumb beneath my swollen eyes.

"You did well tonight," he said softly.

"I fell apart," I whispered.

"No," he corrected. "You gave me everything. That's strength."

My cheeks burned.

He kissed the corner of my mouth. "You obeyed. You trusted me. That's all I ask."

My heart kicked hard at his words, the memory of earlier flickering through my mind like a match struck in the dark.

The blindfold. The slow, deliberate way he made me beg with just his voice and the subtle drag of his fingertips.

The way he teased and denied and edged me until I was trembling—until *I* was the one begging for permission, whispering his name like it was the only word I remembered.

And when he finally gave me what I needed—after I'd begged and pleaded and surrendered fully—I'd come undone so hard I thought I'd never come back.

He had shown me what surrender could feel like.

He had shown me what obedience got me.

And now, wrapped in Egyptian cotton, pressed against the heat of his chest, I wasn't afraid of falling apart anymore.

Because he was right there—waiting to put me back together.

Again and again.

As many times as it took.

CHAPTER 19

I PUSHED HER TOO HARD.

I knew it the moment her tears started—not the overwhelmed kind I'd seen a hundred times before, but something deeper. Fragile. Fractured. Like a dam that had finally burst under too much pressure.

I held her tighter, kissing her temple, her damp cheeks, whispering apologies I wasn't sure she could hear.

It had been stupid of me to assume she wasn't a virgin. I'd suspected, sure—there'd been moments, signs—but she was twenty-one.

Twenty-one and carrying the weight of three lifetimes on her shoulders. I thought maybe the shadows had hardened her into someone who'd already tasted this kind of surrender.

But they hadn't.

And I had fucked her like some starving animal finally let off the leash.

I didn't deserve her.

Now I was still inside her, buried in warmth that had never belonged to anyone else. And I couldn't move. I didn't want to.

My cock nestled deep, but my need wasn't carnal anymore. It was desperate. Protective. Wrecked.

Her body shook with aftershocks—of the scene, the sex, the memory it must have triggered.

She made these soft, broken sounds in her throat that gutted me. Like she didn't even know how to ask for comfort, but her body sought it anyway.

So I gave it.

I curled myself around her, wrapped her in arms twice her size, whispered against her skin as I cleaned her with a warm cloth.

I took my time, careful and reverent, as if maybe I could erase what I'd done—no, not what I'd done, but how unprepared she'd been for it. The strength of the scene.

The way I'd devoured her like she was mine.

She was mine.

But not like that. Not at the cost of her safety. Not if she wasn't ready.

And now? Now she cried into my chest, and I held her tighter, one hand stroking her back while the other cupped the back of her neck.

"I'm so fucking sorry," I breathed. "Mon cœur, I should've known. I should've asked. I should've—God."

She didn't answer.

Just clung to me like a lifeline, like I was the only solid thing in the world she could hold onto.

Her thighs were still sticky with me. Her neck was damp with sweat and tears. Her fingers dug into my side as if afraid I'd vanish.

And the worst part?

Part of me loved it.

The claiming. The closeness. The unbearable intimacy of her cracking open in my arms.

Was I an animal?

Of course.

But not with this woman. Not with the girl who'd let me in, who'd handed over her trust like it weighed nothing when it clearly cost her everything.

Natasha Nash wasn't some weekend submissive.

She wasn't just another scene. She was raw magic wrapped in trauma and razor wire. She needed to be loved like a secret.

Held like a weapon. Touched like she might disappear.

So I held her. All night. I didn't move. Didn't thrust. Didn't fuck.

I just stayed. Buried deep inside the woman who made me feel more human than I had in years.

And when her sobs faded into sleep and her breathing softened, I finally allowed myself to breathe too.

Because she hadn't pushed me away.

Not yet.

And maybe that meant I had a chance to get this right.

～

"No," I whispered, voice rough with emotion. "I'm going to stay inside this little body of yours until you stop running. You're not escaping me tonight."

And just like that, my heart settled.

She was still trembling in my arms, her tears soaking into my skin— not the tears of someone unraveling, but of someone finally letting themselves be held.

Letting the ache break open so it could begin to heal.

"I'm here," I murmured, brushing damp strands of platinum hair away from her face.

Twenty-one, but her eyes held centuries of pain. I should've seen it sooner. Should've recognized the signs.

Should've been gentler with this fractured soul who'd spent a lifetime mistaking survival for peace.

She shook like a frightened bird, and something deep in my chest ached for her. This wasn't just aftercare anymore.

This was something deeper. Something heavier.

Something that made every scene, every contract, every practiced dynamic I'd ever known feel...shallow.

I cleaned her with careful hands, soft cloth, gentle strokes. Every sob was a knife in my chest.

Not because of what we'd done—but because of all the times no one had stayed after. Because of all the nights she'd had to pull herself back together alone.

"Je suis désolé," I whispered against her temple, knowing the words didn't need translation.

Some apologies lived in the silence between heartbeats.

Some healing required touch, not explanation.

She curled into me on instinct, small hands fisting my chest like I was the last solid thing in a world that kept vanishing beneath her feet. And I held her.

Held her like she was mine. Like she'd always been mine.

Not Natasha Nash, not the guarded heir to a crumbling empire. Just a girl in my arms. A girl who deserved softness. Safety. Sleep.

And as our breathing synced—mine steady, hers still catching—I felt it.

My heart, aligning with hers.

Like maybe, just maybe, I was exactly where I was meant to be.

~

THE WINGS SHIMMERED FIRST—GOSSAMER THINGS THAT CAUGHT THE LIGHT when she turned, delicate and ethereal, like they'd been spun from moonlight and whispered secrets.

The short, silvery dress clung to her body like a second skin, dusted with glitter that now lived on her collarbone, her cheeks, her thighs.

Her hair had been braided with little white flowers, loose strands falling around her face like something out of a fever dream.

A fever dream that was mine.

She stood barefoot on the rug, slightly unsure, one hand at her side like she was ready to bolt.

The costume had been Talia's idea—some ridiculous charity masquerade where fairy wings were "mandatory."

But Natasha? She made it look like mythology.

I rose from the couch slowly, devouring her with my eyes. "You know," I said, my voice low. "You keep showing up in my life looking like magic, and I'm starting to think you do it on purpose."

Her cheeks flushed, but she didn't look away. "I feel ridiculous."

"No." I stepped closer. "You look like something out of a dream I'm not supposed to touch."

She gave a shaky little laugh. "And yet..."

My fingers found the curve of her waist. "And yet, here we are."

I didn't kiss her right away. I took my time.

Let my eyes trail down her body, from the glitter smudged over her collarbone to the bare skin of her thighs peeking out beneath the hem.

Her wings twitched slightly when I reached behind her, anchoring my hand to the small of her back.

Then I kissed her.

Slow, deep, reverent—like she was something holy I hadn't believed in until now.

She sighed into me, her hands finding my chest like instinct, like prayer.

86

Her body softened, pressed into mine, and the wings quivered against my arms as I lifted her, setting her on the counter like she weighed nothing.

"I'm not fragile," she whispered against my mouth.

"No," I said, trailing kisses down her throat. "You're feral in glitter and lace."

And then I showed her.

With my hands, my mouth, my body—I showed her that fairy wings didn't make her delicate.

They made her dangerous.

Enchanting.

Mine.

CHAPTER 20
Natasha

THE SHADOWS THAT USUALLY HAUNTED MY NIGHTS WERE EERILY SILENT, AS if they, too, were momentarily appeased by what had just happened.

I lay there, feeling the impossible weight of him—against me, inside me, surrounding me.

Sleep should have been out of reach.

My mind should have been a storm of Mother's taunts, Malcolm's threats, and every demon that normally prowled the edges of my thoughts. But for once, there was only quiet.

Like fresh snow blanketing a battlefield—soft, pure, and oddly comforting in its stillness.

His breath brushed against my neck—steady, sure—anchoring me to this rare moment of peace.

The kind of peace I hadn't even known was possible; the peace that made me understand why people wrote poetry about love, painted sunsets, and chose to keep fighting when the world seemed too dark to bear.

I drifted between wakefulness and dreams, tethered only by the rhythm of his heartbeat pressed close to my back.

No shadows lurked in the corners.

No cruel whispers tore at me. Just silence—deep, beautiful, and sacred.

Time lost all meaning. Hours? Minutes?

I couldn't say how long I lay there, nor did I want to.

Wrapped in Egyptian cotton sheets that probably cost more than my car, held by a man who claimed every fractured piece of me, I felt whole.

And that terrified me more than any nightmare ever had.

Because peace like this came with a price.

Because men like Teo didn't save broken girls like me without wanting something in return. Because the higher you flew, the harder you fell.

But as sleep finally pulled me under, one truth echoed louder than my fear: some falls were worth every painful inch of the descent.

When I woke, the world was quiet except for the steady rhythm of his breathing.

Without a word, he kissed me—deep, demanding, utterly consuming.

He fucked me again and again, each thrust driving away the shadows that clung to my skin. Until I ached with the exquisite pain of being claimed.

Then, without pulling away, he sank deep, his lips finding mine in a fierce, desperate kiss—like he was trying to memorize every part of me, body and soul.

And in that moment, beneath his hands and heat, I forgot fear. Forgot the past.

There was only him. Only this. Only us.

He didn't say a word—just pulled me close, his mouth claiming mine with a hunger that stole my breath.

His hands roamed, urgent and sure, igniting every nerve until the world narrowed to the heat between us.

With every movement, every slow, deliberate touch, he chased the darkness from my skin, replacing it with fire and need.

I trembled beneath him, caught in the fierce rhythm that felt like both punishment and salvation.

When he pressed deeper, his breath ragged against my throat, his lips traced the line of my jaw—soft, fierce, relentless.

In that fierce intimacy, the past dissolved, fear vanished, and all that remained was the raw, electric connection binding us.

It was just him and me—wild, unguarded, utterly alive.

~

"THAT'S MY GIRL, COME TO ME..." TEO'S VOICE WAS LOW AND STEADY, A tether pulling me back from the edge.

I felt like I was about to burst apart from the intensity building inside me.

He gently secured me to the bed, his touch both commanding and careful. Bound and blindfolded, I was completely surrendered—every sense heightened, every nerve alive.

His hands moved with precision, exploring, teasing—sending waves of sensation that left me breathless. He shifted, bringing an unexpected rhythm that sent shivers through me, delicate and urgent.

Every touch, every whisper against my skin, was a promise. A storm and a shelter all at once.

I was overwhelmed—pulled taut between need and release in a way I never thought possible.

~

"WHERE ARE WE?"

I looked around at the butterflies everywhere.

"In a greenhouse. They specifically open this one for butterflies. It's closed this time of year, but I pulled a few strings."

I couldn't look away.

"There's nobody here but us?"

Teo's eyes twinkled as he nodded.

"Whoa," a butterfly landed on my fingertips. I wanted to cry. "They're beautiful."

The entire greenhouse was designed like a zen garden. There was even a tiny bridge with a koi pond. Dangling vines and leaves and larger trees. My eyes trailed over everything feeling calmer than I had in years.

"I thought we could have a picnic," he motioned to his basket. "Here."

I blinked in surprise. "Really?"

"I have snacks." I was wandering over to Teo aware I liked all the odd snacks he brought me. Sensory distractions he said.

I sat across from him on the blanket he laid out in what looked like a lush green patch of grass inside the greenhouse.

"This place is magical," I murmured. In morning sun it looked ethereal.

Teo's smile was unreadable as his eyes filled with banked heat watched me.

"Come here, mon coeur," he murmured as he sat down, stretching his long legs and motioning for me to come on over.

I looked around nervously. "But people—"

"I have the place for the entire day—"

I didn't even want to consider what that meant for me.

"Cameras—"

"There are none. Now come here, ma belle. Or I will get angry."

My heart raced as I crawled a little over into his arms and straddled his lap. Teo's grin was wide and wicked as he held me tighter. His mouth came down on me hungrily as he kissed me picnic basket forgotten.

"Wrap your legs around me."

I did and he nudged me against his erection.

I gasped a little. "Teo."

I had never been out in public like this and even with the greenhouse steamy and foggy and us being some bushes or whatever they were, I didn't feel entirely comfortable.

"It's okay," he murmured. Teo began to play with my nipples and I moaned a little as he tugged the necklace of my dress down. Hiking the skirt of it up higher.

Trembling with need I felt him undoing his belt. His thick cock drawn out as he lifted me up. "Shhh. I have you mon couer, nothing is going to happen to you."

Besides this. Besides him.

I groaned low as he sank me onto him. And then stopped.

A breathless laugh escaped him all teeth and no bite as he smiled.

"Let me in, mon coeur."

"I can't—you're too much—"

"Nonsense," he chuckled. "Come on."

And just like that I whimpered as he slid in. "Oh God. Even that much—"

"You can take me. All of it, mon coeur."

I wanted to scream it felt deliriously good and Teo's eyes lowered, lashes fanning over his cheek bones.

My lips parted over his sinking down some more. Squirming at the stretching. The discomfort that was borderline painful now.

His hands dipped to my nipples playing them as he made out with me.

For long moments I pulsed before sinking down further. It was endless. Adjust. Sink. Adjust. Sink. Until finally he was buried deep in me and I clenched even tighter than ever.

Teo's hands moved around adjust my skirts until it felt like I was locked in the most intimate moment with him.

My legs wrapped around his waist. His forehead pressing to mine.

"Mon coeur."

"Hm?"

He said something that sounded like praise in French. I wasn't good at languages.

"What does that mean?"

"I think I've died and gone to heaven with you."

I laughed lightly feeling him pulsing in me.

"Don't move," I whispered. "I just wanna stay like this."

"Hm, I was hoping you'd say that."

"This was your plan."

I couldn't describe how I felt with him. Nothing came to my mind. Teo kept the shadows at bay. I rock on his length slowly as he played with my hair. Smiling into my lips. His forehead never broke contact with mine.

"Maybe."

I felt a reluctant smile blossom on my lips as I closed my hips rocking my hips a bit more. "Teo—"

"I have you," he groaned shifting me a little so I could be more comfortable. "Just like that."

Teo kissed me like he had all the time in the world—slow, indulgent, and consuming.

Every brush of his lips pulled me deeper under, until I couldn't tell where the hunger ended and the comfort began.

His hands moved with purpose, not demanding, but anchoring—like he was holding me together with every stroke of his fingers.

I didn't even realize I'd torn the dress halfway off until I felt the soft rasp of my bare chest against his still-clothed one. My skin ached for contact. For warmth. For *him.*

I was ice, and he was heat—steady and blazing and mine.

"Shhh," he murmured, voice low, brushing against my ear like a prayer. "I can feel it—don't panic. I'm right here. I've got you."

Then he stripped his shirt off in one fluid motion and pulled me tighter, letting me soak up his heat, his steadiness, until the frantic edge dulled. Until my body stopped trembling.

I exhaled. And moved.

The friction between us was soft at first, almost tentative—my hips gently rolling against him, seeking something wordless and electric.

My clit found the line of his abdomen and every pass sent sparks through my veins. He hissed in a breath but didn't stop me. Just let me take what I needed.

"Teo—" I tried to speak, but the pleasure built too fast, curling through my spine and unraveling everything inside me.

This time, it didn't crash like a wave. It bloomed—warm, expansive, slow like honey—and I gave into it, head tipping back, hair cascading behind me like liquid silver as my body rode the high.

Every breath was a gasp, every grind of my hips a silent plea. His name left my lips in a broken whisper, almost reverent.

I barely registered the sound of his groan or the heat that spilled into me, only the feel of his mouth tracing over my breasts, his tongue flicking a nipple that sent another tremble through my thighs.

When I finally stilled, still straddling him, breath ragged and skin glowing, I dipped my head and kissed him. Gentle. Grateful.

And for the first time, completely present.

But Teo froze.

"What?" I asked, pulling back just enough to see the expression on his face—equal parts awe and amusement.

He tilted his chin toward me, then reached for his phone, quickly flipping it to the front camera and turning the screen toward me.

I blinked. And gasped.

Butterflies.

At least three or four of them had landed in my hair, their delicate wings fluttering with every breath I took.

They perched there like a crown, as if they knew something I didn't.

A breathless laugh escaped me, half in wonder, half in disbelief. "I feel like a princess."

He grinned, tugging me closer, and some of them scattered, but not all. "You look like a queen," he said, his voice hoarse. "*My* queen."

The kiss that followed was slower. Deeper. Not about lust or release—but recognition. A claiming without force. A vow without words.

And this time, when I kissed him back, it wasn't to forget the darkness.

It was to remember the light he'd given me.

CHAPTER 21

Teo

HAVING SEX INSIDE OF A BUTTERFLY GARDEN WASN'T ENOUGH FOR ME.

No. I wanted her everywhere I could get her.

I took her everywhere.

During the week I'd work my ass off. And I spent every single free moment with her. Her...disabilities eased.

With me she was the perfect submissive. I had always wanted to find someone who challenged me and gave me peace in surrender. It brought her peace too. And wasn't that just a fucking dream to me.

Thierry came to see me as a break from his work at Titan.

His future brother-in-law was Reed Whittaker. Adam's older brother and someone I could rarely stand. But if Thierry tolerated him I would too.

"Reed wants me to lead some of Titan," Thierry muttered almost embarrassed.

I grinned. "In Greenwich."

"No," he shook his head, inky black hair so much like mine spilling over. "In Midtown, so I can be closer to mon coeur."

It didn't surprise me we called our women our hearts.

By default, I think the only DuPont born with a heart had been Andrei. But his heart was Talia.

Avani was Thierrys.

And she was mine.

I hadn't told my siblings about my little tete-a-tete with Natasha. I didn't know how to.

Instead I listened to Thierry get excited about his future with Titan. With Avani.

Out of the two of us he had a much harder life I was grateful he didn't remember. He didn't have nightmares. Andrei pulling him out and keeping him close to us kept them at bay.

And he was dating the nicest woman in the world.

My brother had improved.

And I was proud.

"What about you?" He asked innocently. Sometimes Thierry was twenty. Sometimes he was an eight year old curiously asking about my toys.

Ones I didn't share.

"Nothing much." I told him calmly.

"Are you still fucking Lucy Devereaux with her man?"

Ah. That little moment for me had been fun.

But no.

"Lucy loves Adam," I managed. She did. Even when she was with me I saw her texting Adam and missing him. Lucy loved him. No matter what.

My brother's girlfriend was a cupcake.

A metaphorical one at least.

Avani was sweeter than both of the Nash's and the nicest thing around. And I knew Natasha would eat her alive. And the irony was after Drew marrying Talia and me being with Natasha—Avani made sense in the family.

CHAPTER 22
Natasha

THE DOOR CLICKED SHUT BEHIND HIM WITH A FINALITY THAT ECHOED louder than it should've.

I stared at the space he'd just occupied—his coat still draped over the back of the chair, the faint trace of his cologne lingering in the air, like a ghost that refused to leave.

Like him.

And yet...not him.

Because Teo was gone.

And the silence he left behind grew teeth.

My body ached. A good ache, technically. The kind that should've meant something—sore thighs, a tender throat, the raw afterglow of being owned, claimed.

But instead of contentment, a hollow nausea settled in the pit of my stomach.

He'd gotten a call. I'd watched his eyes change—focused, urgent, the brief flicker of apology before he kissed my forehead and said, *"I'll be right back."*

But the door had clicked.

And the quiet didn't feel temporary.

I sat, naked and used, wrapped in one of the cashmere throws he'd ordered for me months ago.

The scent of his skin clung to my sheets. The sheets he'd just fucked me into like I belonged to him.

And maybe I did.

But he'd left.

No bath drawn. No whispered words. No grounding touches.

No aftercare.

Not even a text.

Teo didn't *do* that.

He didn't *leave* after.

Not with me.

Which meant either something was terribly wrong—or I was.

The tremble in my hands wasn't from pleasure.

It was from *everything else.*

My eyes drifted to the nightstand where the contract sat, half-open.

Submission, structure, safety—he'd promised those things. Swore he could handle my sharp edges and soft centers, that he'd hold me together when I unraveled.

But maybe I'd already unraveled, and he just didn't want to pick up the pieces anymore.

I tried to breathe. In through the nose, out through the mouth.

Like my therapist taught me.

But my throat tightened. My chest caved in.

It started with a whimper. A small, traitorous sound in the back of my throat.

And then came the shake. The kind of trembling that started in my fingertips and spread like static.

I curled into myself on the bed, knees to chest, my entire frame folding in like a paper bird under too much pressure.

He didn't mean to hurt me.

He probably didn't even *know.*

But that didn't matter. Because the monster in my head—the one that wore my mother's perfume and Malcolm's watch—told me everything I needed to know:

You were too much again.

You scared him off.

Even he doesn't want you like this.

I pressed the heels of my palms into my eyes until white spots bloomed behind my lids.

I wanted to scream.

I wanted to vanish.

I wanted him back.

I crawled out of bed and stumbled to the bathroom. My knees hit tile and I didn't even feel it.

I turned the water on too hot and stepped under it anyway.

Let it sting.

Let it punish.

Let it silence the echo of that door closing.

My skin burned. My bones ached.

And the sob that finally escaped wasn't pretty or cinematic. It was animal. Deep and broken and *real*.

I didn't cry because he left.

I cried because it confirmed what I feared most.

Even love—with all its structure and silk sheets and whispered French —wasn't enough to fix me.

I was still the girl in the wreckage. Still the daughter no one could love.

Still Natasha Nash.

Too much.

Too fragile.

Too fucked up to keep.

I told myself I was fine.

That I didn't need a man to hold me after.

That I wasn't some fragile porcelain thing, cracked and waiting to shatter.

But the lies curdled in my mouth, thick and sour and choking.

I curled tighter into myself, arms wrapped around my knees, forehead pressed to trembling thighs. Trying to contain it. Trying to keep the storm inside.

A whimper slipped out—small, high-pitched, pathetic. Like a wounded animal too tired to run.

It startled even me.

What did I do wrong?

He said I'd been good.

He'd looked at me like I mattered. Touched me like I was something precious.

His.

He kissed me like he could taste the pieces no one else had cared to find.

So why did it feel like abandonment?

The shadows didn't wait for nightfall this time.

They came clawing through the cracks in my ribs.

They wore my mother's perfume and my father's silence.

They spoke in Malcolm's voice and sat in the empty spaces Teo had just left behind.

They told me the truth.

Worthless, Natasha.

Useless.

You ruin everything you touch.

I pressed the heels of my hands into my eyes until stars burst behind my eyelids.

I needed something. Anything.

But the thought of reaching out—of calling him—made my stomach twist.

Because that would make it *real*.

That I was weak.

That I was the clingy one.

That I was too much. Again.

I tried to stand, but my legs buckled. The ache between them pulsed, sharp and unmistakable.

I welcomed it.

I *deserved* it.

The punishment for believing, even for a moment, that I could have something good.

I crawled—humiliated and naked—into the bathroom, dragging the cashmere throw behind me like a broken flag.

The water scalded when it hit my skin, but I didn't move. Didn't flinch.

I just folded myself into the corner of the shower, arms wrapped around my stomach, forehead against the tile, and let it burn.

Let it *cleanse*.

Let it strip away the guilt and the shame and the stupid, naive hope that someone like me could be loved without condition.

But it didn't.

It never did.

When the sob came, it wasn't elegant.

It didn't roll down my cheeks like some tragic movie heroine.

It was ripped from somewhere deep in my chest.

Animal.

Ragged.

Real.

I screamed into my towel.

Bit down until I tasted copper.

Curled into the cold tile and shook so hard my teeth clattered.

I didn't want him for sex.

I didn't want him to fix me.

I just wanted...*him.* His voice. His steadiness. That tether he gave me when my mind slipped too far into the dark.

I just wanted him to come back.

To see me like this and not run.

To pull me into his arms and whisper, *I've got you, mon cœur. I'm here.*

But he was gone.

And maybe I was too much. Even for him.

Even for a man who fucked like sin and spoke like salvation.

Maybe love was just a leash people yanked when they wanted something.

Maybe this was what I got for asking for more than scraps.

The shadows wrapped around me like a second skin.

And when they started whispering again, I didn't fight them.

I listened.

Because they sounded like the truth.

CHAPTER 23

I'D ASKED THE SECRETARY TO CALL ME THE MOMENT SHE NOTICED NATASHA looking off—blank-eyed, brittle, like she might shatter under the weight of something invisible. When the call came, I left my meeting mid-sentence. I didn't explain. Didn't have to.

Now she was in my arms, and I was furious. Not at her. At myself.

I should've known.

I should've seen it earlier.

She trembled as I shifted her weight, unlocking my penthouse with one hand and nudging the door open with my shoulder. The place was warm, dimly lit. No sharp corners. I'd had it prepared for her—just in case.

I carried her straight to my bedroom and sat on the edge of the bed, cradling her in my lap like a doll someone had loved too hard.

She curled into me. Small. Quiet. Cold.

"I've got you," I whispered into her hair. "I've got you, mon cœur."

No response.

I tugged the cashmere blanket over her shoulders, holding her against my chest. I didn't undress her. Didn't ask her to talk. Just held her. Rocked her, barely moving. Let her breathing guide mine until the tremors began to slow.

Her fingers gripped my shirt weakly, like she wasn't even aware of doing it.

I texted Jace with my free hand:

> Assemble a team for IT and international expansion. Prioritize discretion. NDA level black. I want eyes on everyone who touches her name.

He responded instantly:

> Already pulling personnel from London and Zurich. You want them briefed tonight?

> Tomorrow morning. Focus on her digital footprint. I want everything buried. And start vetting a private trauma therapist. Not the ones who write memoirs. The kind who fix ghosts.

My attention flicked back to her when I felt wetness seeping into my collar.

Tears. Silent ones.

She still hadn't said a word.

"Shh," I murmured, brushing her damp cheek. "You don't have to hold it together. Not with me."

She shuddered. "I-I thought I was okay."

"You don't have to be okay. You just have to be here."

"I broke." Her voice cracked, small and hollow. "And you weren't there."

I closed my eyes against the guilt.

That was the thing about women like her—strong, scarred, always bracing for the blow. They didn't ask for help.

They just collapsed quietly, hoping no one noticed the ruin.

"I'm here now." I pressed my lips to her temple. "And I'm not going anywhere."

"I didn't want to need you." A sob slipped out before she could catch it. "But I do."

"Good." I eased us back into the pillows, keeping her wrapped against me. "Because I need you too. And I'm not ashamed of that."

We lay like that for a long time—her heart pounding wild and broken against my chest, mine a steady drum beneath hers.

Eventually, when her sobs turned to hiccups, I pulled her blanket tighter and whispered, "Sleep. I'll keep watch."

She didn't answer, but her fingers curled tighter in my shirt. Like a silent agreement. Like trust.

Like home.

CHAPTER 24
Natasha

I didn't like the blindfold.

No, I hated it.

"I can't—" I panted struggling. "I can't. Please—"

"Tell me what you need."

"Your eyes." It came through with zero hesitation. I needed to see him. Needed to feel those blues watching me.

He quickly removed it and I arched into his touch craving him. My lashes fluttered as I calmed down watching him.

"Need me?" I nodded unable to speak as his lips moved over mine. His tongue darting out to lick my lips. "Is that better?"

"Yes." It was barely a fucking whisper leaving me as I felt his hand snaking down to push that vibrator deeper. He hadn't even turned it on and I was already melting.

"Clench down."

I did closing my eyes to the thick sensation.

"Clench again."

I did.

"Breathe."

I obeyed feeling helpless. Tied up. At his mercy. And there had never been so much relief. Not once.

Hanging on the edge with him felt different.

I could only whisper in that moment.

"Teo."

"Yes, mon coeur?"

"What are you doing?"

"I was hoping to calm you down. Maybe teach you a lesson," his dark whisper sank somewhere deep in me.

And then he turned on the vibrator.

I spasmed instantly closing my eyes tugging against the restraints as Teo whispered into my mouth. "Shhh. It's okay, mon coeur. It's okay."

It wasn't. I could feel it deep inside of me thrumming wildly against that spot.

I began to squirm almost instantly but the restraints held me in place as Teo fidgeted with part of it and I knew what he was trying to do even before he did. He was adjusting the part that went over my clit.

But instead of putting it there?

He adjusted it to just a little over it and around it. I bucked my hips to no avail. Teo chuckled darkly over my mouth.

"Painful?"

"No." I couldn't stop my hips from working to take it more. Right there. So close.

But it wouldn't budge. A frustrated noise left me.

"No, you don't get to move, mon coeur," he whispered. "Not an inch." I gasped as it lodged deeper as I clenched.

"Oh God," I whimpered.

"I know, it won't hurt if you give in. Clench down."

My body wasn't my own. I was convinced he'd done something to me to get me to obey him.

"There you go, it's easier this way, hm?"

I whimpered frustrated, gripping the restraints and clawing at it. My legs kept far enough to not clench, and wide enough for him to play with me.

Teo's hand came up to tug at one of my nipples, his mouth dipping to the other one.

Wet hot heat met sensitized flesh and I arched.

And then, for searing moments, it was all burning-hot pleasure—sharp, bright, relentless.

I kept clenching around nothing, and the toy kept pressing against that maddening spot, pulsing with a rhythm that almost—but not quite—matched my own. My body was straining, trying to get there, to catch the edge of release, but it kept slipping away like a cruel mirage.

I was thrashing or trying to, my fingers tangled in the sheets, my thighs twitching in protest. Teo stayed beside me, calm and maddeningly composed, braced on one elbow like he was watching a work of art come alive beneath his hands.

His smirk was all sin. "There you go. Keep going, mon cœur."

I gasped, arching hard. "I can't—" The frustration bled into my voice. I felt...helpless. Stranded. Raw.

"Yes, you can," he said softly, and somehow that made it worse. Or better. Or both.

"How?" I nearly whimpered, breath catching on every pulse of sensation. "It's right there and I—"

"When I tell you," he murmured, voice low and dark, curling through me like smoke. "You'll come when I say. Not before."

God, he was *devious*. Wicked. In control of every thread unraveling inside me.

"Watch."

His hand cupped my breast, fingers teasing the sensitive peak until I gasped.

Then his mouth followed—hot, firm, purposeful—sucking until the tension low in my belly turned molten. His other hand moved between my legs again, adjusting the angle of the toy, just slightly, *perfectly*.

Then his mouth found mine again, tongue thrusting in lazy, possessive strokes that mimicked what I wanted most.

I felt caged by my own pleasure, pinned between the heat of his body and the unbearable sweetness of not being allowed to let go.

"Such a good girl," he whispered between kisses. "So close. So desperate."

I moaned, desperate was an understatement.

He chuckled darkly, mouth dragging along my jaw. "You feel how soaked you are for me? How perfect this is? All mine."

I was panting now, barely holding on.

My body begged for permission while my mind spiraled, caught in the exquisite cruelty of his control. My nails bit into his back. "Teo—please—"

"Almost." He brushed his lips over my ear. "I want you trembling when I say it. I want to feel you fall apart."

I whimpered as the pleasure built again, coiling tighter and tighter.

He kissed me again, slower this time, his tongue licking into me like he owned me—like he *already* had.

And when his voice finally came again, gravel-warm and absolute, it shattered everything.

"Now, mon cœur. Now."

And I *broke* for him.

THE SILENCE AFTER FELT DEEPER THAN SLEEP.

My body trembled—not from pleasure anymore, but from something quieter. Something that crawled out from under my ribs when the fire had gone out.

I turned my face away, ashamed of how hard I'd clung to him, how easily I'd come undone for someone who could so easily break me.

He didn't let me turn far.

Teo's arms closed around me like a promise. Not a demand. Not possession. Just...presence.

"Hey," he murmured, breath brushing the shell of my ear. "Still with me?"

I nodded, or tried to. My throat was tight. My skin too thin.

He reached over the edge of the bed and pulled a blanket up over both of us, even though I was burning.

Even though my chest felt cracked open, raw and exposed in ways I hadn't expected.

"I'm sorry," I whispered.

"For what?"

"For..." I didn't even know. "Needing you like that."

His grip tightened just a little, grounding. "Mon cœur. I *want* to be needed."

"But I'm a mess," I said, voice small. "You don't even know the half of it. I fall apart like it's a part-time job."

"Then let me clock in."

That startled a quiet laugh out of me. It wasn't much, but it was real.

He kissed my forehead—soft, slow, reverent.

"You think I didn't notice the way you fight to hold it all together? You're not weak for needing rest. Or comfort. Or someone who gives a damn."

I turned my face into his chest and finally let myself breathe. Let myself be held.

107

No games. No expectations. Just...this.

His fingers brushed through my hair, over and over, until my shaking eased.

Until the echoes of old panic faded into something distant, something I could look at without drowning.

"You didn't break me," I whispered.

His voice was thick when he answered. "Good. Because I never want to be the reason you shatter."

We stayed like that, tangled in quiet. Nothing explosive. Nothing loud. Just skin to skin and heartbeat to heartbeat.

And for the first time in a long time, I didn't feel like I was bracing for impact.

I just felt...safe.

CHAPTER 25

Tea

I DIDN'T KNOW WHAT ELSE TO DO.

She was unraveling in front of me—bit by bit, breath by breath—like a thread being pulled too tight until the entire fabric frayed.

One minute she was quiet. Too quiet. Curled into herself on the couch with her knees tucked under her chin, staring at something I couldn't see. And the next...she was shaking. Mumbling things that didn't make sense. Asking questions I couldn't answer—like how many times the elevator had stopped. Like whether her sister was alive. Like whether she'd died and no one told her.

She wasn't making jokes anymore.

She wasn't even *present*.

The lights were on, but no one was home.

And I—Mr. Control, Mr. Fix-It, Mr. Fucking Durand—was out of options.

I'd held her through panic attacks. I'd stayed up with her during night terrors, whispered her through the worst of the flashbacks. But this wasn't that. This wasn't a single storm. This was a flood.

She hadn't eaten in days. Hadn't slept more than an hour at a time. Hadn't spoken a full sentence in the last twenty-four hours that didn't include the word *sorry*.

And somewhere between watching her take her third shower in one night and finding her sitting in the hallway in nothing but a T-shirt and wet hair, I realized something was *very* wrong.

This wasn't grief. This wasn't anxiety.

This was a relapse.

This was a spiral.

This was the woman I love—my *mon cœur*—slipping through my fingers.

So I made the call.

I wrapped her in a blanket she barely noticed and carried her to the car. She didn't fight me. That's how I knew it was bad. She just leaned into me like she was exhausted by her own existence, like she didn't trust her legs to carry her anymore.

She kept whispering things under her breath—phrases that made no sense until you lined them up next to the trauma.

"Don't put the knife down."

"She won't stop laughing."

"I don't want the shadows to win."

I kept one hand on the wheel and one on her knee, anchoring her with my touch like I had in the elevator. But this wasn't a confined space or a passing moment. This was her mind—open, bleeding, and begging for relief.

I hated the hospital. Hated what it represented. But I hated this more.

I loved her.

But love wasn't enough to fix this.

So I drove.

Because sometimes the strongest thing you can do for someone you love is admit you can't save them on your own.

And right now, Natasha needed more than me.

She needed help.

And I wasn't going to lose her to the shadows. Not without a fight.

THE WHEELS HUMMED AGAINST THE PAVEMENT, THE WORLD OUTSIDE swallowed by night. City lights gave way to open stretches of dark road, neon signs flickering like ghosts in the distance. She hadn't spoken since we left the building, her legs curled under her in the passenger seat, head leaning against the cool glass.

Every so often I'd glance over, just to make sure she was still breathing.

"Hungry?" I asked finally, voice low. It felt like shouting in the silence between us.

She didn't answer right away. Her eyes stayed on the road ahead, distant and glazed. Then, a slight nod. "I could eat."

I turned off at the next exit, pulled into a twenty-four-hour diner that looked like it hadn't changed since 1982. Fluorescent lights buzzed overhead, the parking lot nearly empty except for a beat-up pickup and a delivery van.

Inside, it smelled like bacon grease and burnt coffee. I watched her closely as we walked in—how her shoulders tensed when the bell over the door rang, how she automatically chose the booth farthest from the windows, her back to the wall. Always facing the exits. Always scanning.

A waitress with smeared lipstick and tired eyes handed us menus. I ordered for both of us. She didn't object.

The silence stretched between us like taut wire. She stirred her coffee without drinking it, fingers trembling faintly.

"You ever do this before?" I asked.

She blinked. "Eat?"

"Eat with someone. Late night drive. Empty diner. It feels...cinematic."

Her lips curved slightly. Almost a smile. "I don't think I've ever been someone's late-night drive."

"You're mine."

Her gaze shot up to meet mine, sharp and startled.

"I didn't mean—" I ran a hand through my hair. "I meant tonight. You're mine tonight. In the car. At the booth. That's all."

She stared at me like she was trying to solve a puzzle with missing pieces. Then, softly, "Why are you being so nice to me?"

I leaned back in the booth, elbows on the table. "Because you're tired. Because you haven't eaten in days. Because when you scream in your sleep, I hear it. Because you don't ask for help, and it's fucking killing me to watch you pretend you don't need it."

She looked away again. Her coffee was still untouched.

I hesitated before adding, "And because I want you to know what it feels like to be taken care of."

Silence.

Then, almost too soft to hear, "I don't know what to do with that."

"I'll show you," I said. "One fry at a time."

She actually laughed—quiet and broken, but real.

And for the first time all night, the shadows around her seemed to pull back.

Just a little.

Just enough.

And maybe that was all we needed.

For now.

∾

THE HAWAIIAN-THEMED PLACE WAS KITSCHY IN A WAY I WOULDN'T USUALLY tolerate—tiki torches at the entrance, ukulele music playing over cheap speakers, pineapple-shaped drink glasses—but she smiled when she saw it.

So we stayed.

Inside, the air smelled like grilled meat, sugar, and something floral that clung to the waitstaff's leis. String lights twinkled above the booths, casting soft shadows.

It was full of loud laughter and messy plates and children playing under tables, and somehow—somehow—it didn't make her flinch.

"You okay?" I asked quietly as we slid into a booth. The vinyl squeaked under us.

She nodded, eyes scanning the room. "Yeah. It's...familiar. Not exactly this, but...close."

I didn't ask what she meant. She'd tell me if she wanted to.

Our waitress was chipper, all sunshine and freckles, and Natasha didn't shy away when she addressed her. She even smiled—nervous and barely there, but it still counted.

She ordered the loco moco. I got the kalua pork plate. She scrunched her nose when I told her I wanted Spam musubi too.

"That's disgusting," she said, but there was laughter in her voice.

I leaned back in the booth and watched her more than I should have. "You say that like you didn't eat pickles and peanut butter at two in the morning last week."

She blinked. "You weren't supposed to see that."

"I see everything."

She blushed then, cheeks coloring soft pink under the warm glow of the lights. "Shut up."

I didn't. Couldn't. I reached across the table and hooked my pinky through hers. It wasn't dramatic or possessive. It was just contact. Quiet, warm, and a little terrifying.

"This is nice," she said after a long pause, almost surprised.

"It is."

"I don't do nice."

I smiled. "You're doing it now."

She ducked her head. "I don't trust it. Like the universe is about to punish me for feeling good."

"I'll fight the universe if it tries."

She looked up, caught off guard by the intensity in my voice. Her lips parted like she wanted to say something, but didn't.

Dinner came in steaming, chaotic waves—bowls of rice, pulled pork, runny egg over beef patties, mac salad in chipped ceramic. She ate slowly, savoring each bite like it might disappear if she moved too fast. It made something in my chest ache.

"You ever go to places like this growing up?" I asked, just to keep her here in the now.

She paused mid-bite. "No. My mother thought anything casual was low-class. We weren't allowed to eat with our hands, let alone at a place where they served food in baskets."

"So this is rebellion?"

"Massive rebellion," she said, deadpan. "Eggs and gravy over hamburger steak. I'm practically a war criminal."

She smiled at me again, small and shy.

And something about that look—daisies in a field, sunlight through blinds, that kind of fragile beauty—made me want to take her home and wrap her in a blanket until the world stopped hurting.

We didn't talk about the business. Or the trauma. Or the way she still sometimes cried in her sleep.

We just sat there, sharing food and quiet jokes, my pinky still looped around hers like it anchored us both.

And for a few moments, it didn't feel like survival.

It felt like something else.

Maybe even something close to love.

CHAPTER 26
Natasha

THE SCENT OF DAISIES HIT ME FIRST WHEN TEO CAME HOME—FRESH AND pure, like the first flowers he'd ever sent me. Innocent. Hopeful. A promise.

He moved through my apartment like he'd always belonged there, like this wasn't something borrowed or breakable.

His presence filled the space without crowding it—quiet, measured grace that made chaos seem optional, like I could choose peace if I just stayed near him.

He set the takeout down on the counter like it was muscle memory, like we did this every night—except we didn't. Not really.

We existed in stolen moments, in breathless hours between break-downs and recoveries. But he made it feel like forever.

Like permanence. Like I could let my guard down without the world punishing me for it.

He didn't even glance at the food. That's how I knew.

It wasn't about dinner. It wasn't about comfort. It wasn't even about pretending.

Something was wrong.

Something in the way he moved—the slight drag of his hand across the counter, the extra second he stood there without turning around—told me he wasn't here just to feed me or fuck me or keep me company.

Something was unraveling behind his eyes, something he was trying too hard to hide under stillness and certainty.

And I felt my chest tighten.

Because I knew this version of him.

The version who came bearing calm like a gift he didn't know how to wrap. The version who kissed my forehead before delivering a blow.

I watched from the doorway, suddenly too aware of the silence between us. It wasn't cold. It wasn't even distant.

It was anticipatory.

The kind of silence that came before a storm.

And maybe that's what scared me the most—that he still moved through my life like he belonged in it, even if he was about to take something away.

Even if I was about to break.

Again.

"Come here, *mon cœur*," he murmured.

And like always, I went.

Because I always went.

His hand was warm in mine, grounding me in the present, even when my past never really let me stay there.

Those impossible blue eyes—like storms over still water—met mine, but there was something unreadable behind them tonight. Something heavy. Decided.

His kiss was different. Slower. Deeper.

Not lust. Not hunger.

Memorization.

I should have known. I should have *known*.

But his hands on my skin made thinking impossible.

And when his body covered mine, when we moved in rhythm, it felt like maybe—just maybe—he saw me. Wanted me.

Not the legacy. Not the name. *Me*.

Later, tangled in the sheets that smelled of sandalwood and sex and *him*, he traced gentle circles on my bare shoulder.

"I need to tell you something."

The room shifted.

The shadows in the corner stirred like they always did when the air changed—sensing my dread before I did.

"What is it?" I asked, too soft. Too late.

He didn't move. Didn't leave my body. Stayed buried inside me like it would anchor the words, soften the blow.

"I've spoken with Andrei about Nash Group."

I stilled. Every cell in my body froze.

"What about it?"

"The company needs to be absorbed into Durand Industries."

Each word fell like a blade.

Clean. Precise. Fatal.

"You won't need to continue CEO training."

And just like that, the walls shattered.

The moment collapsed into memory—glass, blood, her laughter as the car burned. Camilla's voice sliced through time like a ghost with teeth.

Worthless.

Broken.

Useless.

"Get off me!" I screamed, shoving at his chest. The peace we'd built between bodies, between breaths, splintered into pure terror.

"Mon cœur, wait—"

But I was already gone. Lost in the wreckage.

Metal screaming.

Glass in my skin.

Mother laughing as she walked away from the flames.

Teo moved instinctively, pinning me down—not to hurt, but to protect. His body covering mine as I thrashed beneath him, sobbing, trembling, unraveling.

"You're having a panic attack," he said firmly, his voice cleaving through the chaos. "Breathe with me."

"I can't—" The words broke between sobs. "I can't do anything right. Never good enough. Never—"

"Listen to my voice," he commanded, unwavering.

Can't even walk right. Now you can't even run a company.

"She was right," I choked out. "I'm nothing—"

"Non." His voice dropped, darker, fiercer. "You're mine. And I won't let her win."

But the shadows kept pressing, and now they wore Malcolm's face—gun pointed at Talia, my finger on the trigger.

"I'll fail," I sobbed. "Like I failed him. Like I fail everyone—"

"You saved Talia." His lips brushed my temple. "You protect the ones you love. That's not failure. That's *grace.*"

Still, I shook beneath him, sobs wracking my ribs. "I don't know how to be *nothing*."

"You're not nothing." His weight shifted, cradling me now, holding me instead of restraining. "You're *everything*. My everything."

"It's okay," he whispered again.

It's not okay.

I couldn't stop shaking. Couldn't stop clawing at his chest like I wanted to draw blood.

"You did this to me!" I screamed.

"Because I *love* you!" The words tore out of him—raw, loud, and almost angry.

I froze.

The silence that followed was deafening. The truth of it vibrated in the space between us like a fault line.

"I love you too much to watch you destroy yourself just to prove something," he said into the silence. "You're not a leader. You're not a follower. You're just...existing. And it's killing you."

I couldn't breathe. Could barely listen.

He kept going, voice thick and low. "You feel safer on a beach. Or at home. Or in a goddamn garden, watching butterflies. Do you understand me?"

I didn't.

I didn't understand how someone could love all the parts of me I'd been taught to hide. To loathe.

I didn't understand why the part of me that used to crave power now just...wanted to be held.

Six Years Later

MATTEO

DINNER AT THE MATTISON HOME WAS WILD.

To say the least.

Avani had kids. Talia had Drew. Little Drew was five. And Avani's baby Theo was turning one.

And mine was four.

"*Papa.*"

"Yes, mon ange," I scooped up one of my four year old twins in my arms. The other one was no doubt still in the bathroom with his mother, but the moment Nikolai heard me walking in he ran to me.

Naked.

Soaking wet.

Giggling up a storm.

"Papa!"

"Yes," I laughed as Natasha shouted something from the bathroom and I quickly bundled him up.

She was holding his brother Luke in her arms puffing out a breath. "He ran off."

I bit back my laughter figuring it would encourage the boys so I forced myself to sternly eye both of them now grinning ear to ear.

"You two troublemakers causing *Maman* grief?"

Both of them shook their heads as Natasha and I bundled them up and took them into the bedroom. They were like wet eels out of the bathroom and Natasha and I laughed as we got them into their pajamas and in bed.

The twins shared a room for now but eventually we'd split them up if they wanted it.

"Mrs. DuPont," I murmured.

She sighed in my arms. "Drew was over earlier with Talia and they had a blast with Theo and Ty."

Avani and Thierry had two boys, and a little girl on the way.

I had never even heard of a girl being born in our family and Thierry was freaking out.

"I'm borrowing a Titan," I murmured. "Thierry says he's good."

"This is Landon," Thierry motioned to his employee. "He's a Titan and he recently took over for Nathan Wyatt. He'll be helping you if you two need a guard."

My wife was pregnant again and she needed a bodyguard at her side. To say life had been kind to us had been a light statement.

I was running Roadsters from the side while Natasha stayed at home. To say I was happy was an understatement.

Of the year.

I was happier than I could have been.

The reformed sinner turned husband.

The lover turned loyal.

And a DuPont who found his match.

Debrief

You have successfully completed your final mission at Titan Security with the last book in the entire saga.

Teo and Nat were such a fucking wonder to write, but I will definitely miss everyone else.

Titan Security, Underworld Kings, Midnight Gods, was my year long project to get done right—and I did it!

Hooray!
Congrats.
And thank you for reading.

Your Mission Is Over

Stroke of Luck

CHAPTER ONE — EXCERPT

I was going to throw my drink at the sleazy Suit and Tie with a cocky smirk, his wedding ring glinting under the club lights.

"Let me take you home tonight."

Biting back a comment, I tried not to let it grate on my nerves that it was because of men like Suit and Tie over here that I was bringing in my twenty-fifth birthday today, a virgin.

Instead of blaming it on life, a tiny dating pool filled with arseholes, and the responsibilities that consumed me?

My frustrations were on this idiot.

I had come to Teasers, one of New York's premier burlesque clubs, intending to escape.

Around me, the 1920's style decor, with floating multi-colored parasol umbrellas and lush, warm lighting, created a wonderland for seduction.

Scantily-clad performers in colorful wings, lingerie meant to be torn off with guests, and feather boas wrapped around their necks—I would have been in girl heaven.

The scent of white sage and flowers from the live plants mingled in the air, usually a comfort—now tainted by Suit and Tie's cheap cologne. Fidgeting with the vines dangling near my shoulder, I leaned back against the plush velvet barstool, trying to maintain distance.

"No, thank you," I replied firmly, but his eyes only widened, his smirk growing.

"Goddamn, your accent is sexy," he was undeterred.

"I'm waiting for someone." *Anyone. But you.*

As he reached out, I scooted further back, but before I could react, a figure in black obstructed my view.

The unmistakable scent of sea and spice filled my senses, and for a moment, I shifted in my seat, my heart pounding.

Reed Whittaker, CEO of Titan Security and the source of all my sexual frustration for the last three years, blocked my view. Broad shoulders. Chocolate hair.

The kind of look that made a woman think twice about her late-night decisions.

"Not gonna happen," Reed rumbled, his rich, velvety baritone laced with quiet menace.

The Suit and Tie sounded offended, his bravado deflating. "Who the fuck are you?"

"Don't even think about it," Reed said in a voice I heard over the music. "Turn around, go back to your friends."

Reed cut an intimidatingly rugged figure even among the common masses, exuding an undercurrent of raw power usually reserved for archangels strolling among humans.

The aura of intensity radiated from him.

Reed liked to make the occasional unannounced visit to Teasers, and by some stroke of luck, I seemed to be there on those nights.

His focus remained fixed on me the nights he was here, ensuring my safety even when I hadn't realized I needed protection.

But I figured that was his job. I told myself it wasn't a big deal. He'd usher me into cabs, steadying me with those large, calloused hands.

Except for that one night months ago when a friend's early departure prompted my exit shortly after.

As I approached the entrance, Reed materialized from the shadows.

Is everything all right? Is there anyone taking you home?...I can.

Why? I can catch a cab...

I just want to make sure you get home safe. Can I do that?

Sure...

Reed walked me to my doorstep, remaining in the hall until I was safely inside.

The entire interaction burned itself into my consciousness. Just a man ensuring a woman's safe passage home. Even though I hadn't so much as touched a drop at the club that night, the memory alone intoxicated me for weeks afterward.

He wanted to make sure I was safe. Without touching me. He never pushed for more.

Almost like he waited until I was comfortable.

A warm heat blossomed within me that had nothing to do with filling any empty space. Just his mere existence was enough to set me alight.

Because I wanted Reed. Lara confided that she trusted him implicitly to protect everyone.

Reed took that responsibility seriously.

I didn't hear what Suit and Tie said to Reed.

He was sputtering before Reed, and even surrounded by the dancers, every eye around me in the club seemed inexplicably drawn to this. Suit and Tie grumbled something under his breath.

The taut line of Reed's shoulders tensed like he was physically restraining himself.

"I'm not going to repeat myself. Get out. Or you can get kicked out."

"Yeah, and who the fuck are you?"

I saw the way Reed's entire body stiffened. *Drat.*

Before I could overthink it, I reacted on sheer instinct. I don't know what possessed me then, but I felt the dangerous shift as Reed tipped his head, his body coiling.

On instinct, I reached out, and my hand found its way into his. "Reed."

The instant we made contact, he looked over his shoulder at me, those storm-cloud eyes flashing with an untamed intensity that stole my breath.

I shook my head slightly, silently pleading. Unspeakable emotions lingered in his gaze as it raked over me with heat.

I injected some tease into my voice. "Where have you been? I've been waiting for you." *In more ways than one.*

His brow furrowed a fraction, and I willed him with my eyes to just go along with it.

Please, just play along. He searched my face intently.

When his head swung back towards the hapless suit, Reed was every inch the merciless predator, catching the attention of the rest of the club's security.

One of them, Nate Wyatt, a blonde Viking of a man, emerged soundlessly to stand at Reed's side.

Unlike Reed, Nate wore a shirt that said "Security" on the back.

Though not as massively built as Reed's, Nate's broad shoulders and navy eyes radiated an equal aura of threat.

He took one look at the slime ball, not hesitating in the slightest to reach out and lift him bodily from his seat.

I was too stunned to speak, unconsciously gripping Reed's hand.

A silent look passed between Nate and Reed, and whatever he saw in his boss's eyes made Nate shake his head at the suit, almost sympathetically.

I held my breath as the man squawked indignantly about harassment and lawsuits.

Nate all but growled, flanked by two other immense security guards, forcibly ejecting not just Suit and Tie, but his entire friend group. All because of me.

Embarrassment flooded me as I tried to tug my hand back from Reed's grip.

But he wouldn't release me, as his eyes followed his men until they disappeared from view, seemingly oblivious to the murmuring crowd we had attracted.

Reed loosened his grip, though his fingers remained tangled with mine.

"Don't feel bad," he said evenly, as though dealing with such confrontations was all in a night's work for him.

Tousled chocolate hair, just messy enough to tempt wandering fingers. A jawline perpetually tense.

Clean-shaven and smelling like the sea, Reed Whittaker was the kind of man who made women rethink their decisions. Several times.

He towered over my frame, forcing me to tip my head back to meet that stormy gaze head-on from where I sat.

Reed fit the dark, seductive aesthetic of the club like he was born to it.

He ran Teasers security with an iron fist, yet he moved through the crowd with an ease, a comfort of knowing he was in charge.

Everyone yielded to him.

He didn't dress the part of a CEO, his classic bomber jacket over a white shirt.

Powerfully built, the loose material hinted at the sinewy muscles beneath.

My imagination ran wild with visions of him making love to me beneath the cascading waterfall installation or near the canopy of pink cherry blossoms draped over the mezzanine.

He made me feel a little unhinged, untamed.

A little out of it.

Growing up with a Bengali-English mother and an English father, my baby sister Avani and I had inherited a blend of mannerisms and cultural practices from our parents.

Once, I landed in Reed's arms when I nearly took a spill months ago.

Reed had materialized by my side with lightning-fast reflexes, one broad palm across the small of my back, catching me against his solid chest before I could fall.

I still remember covering my burning face with a hand and murmuring an embarrassed thanks, unconsciously dipping into a tiny, deferential bow of gratitude.

A habit ingrained from my Mum.

When I finally peeked up at him through my lashes, Reed's lips curved into an amused smile that set my olive skin ablaze with a crimson flush.

My friends loved to tease me about my not-so-subtle fixation on Reed, which I staunchly denied.

After all, I had an obligation to Avani to not parade a revolving cast of potential lovers before her.

To my sister, I was already unconventional as a pseudo-parent.

Being a successful social media influencer, I'd been so focused on raising Avani and running my business that I neglected my own needs and desires.

Dating was one realm of life I had no experience navigating. Men were a no-go.

The influencer life was less glamorous than people thought, and it had left me feeling emptier than I wanted to feel. Which led me to Teasers tonight. Desperate to no longer feel so stuck.

Privately dreaming of Reed showing me what I'd been missing. Wondering if the reality could possibly live up to the fantasies.

"Are you all right?" The rough timbre of Reed's voice dragged me from my wandering thoughts.

That familiar clench of his jaw, the storm brewing in his eyes.

It paralyzed me every time our paths crossed.

I had barely exchanged words with him, yet the charged silence crackled, threatening to consume me if he so much as brushed against me.

I blamed it on the pent-up energy and not because Reed was well...Reed.

"You didn't have to do all that," I managed, shaking my head minutely. "I didn't want to make a scene."

"You didn't make a scene," Reed's deep voice washed over me as he stated the obvious with maddening calm. "I did."

Reed was a looming storm.

The stillness before the lightning cracked through the sky. I told myself the fluttering in my ribcage was simply the effects of too many mojitos consumed too quickly on an empty stomach.

"Does that happen to you often?"

It did. More than he knew.

The overzealous fans at meet and greets. The creepy comments on my Instagram and social media in general.

Pinned by the weight of his stare, I didn't know how to answer him. Something lurked under his surface, something that told me he hadn't stopped thinking about what he'd like to do to Suit and Tie.

"It's all right."

"It's not alright. He shouldn't have tried to put his hands on you," Reed's eyes darkened as he bit out the words. He raked over the slinky dress, hugging my curves before snagging on my heels.

"He didn't—"

"He was going to," Reed stated. "That was enough."

"Enough?" I repeated.

Reed's face remained impassive. "Why did you hold me back?" Storm cloud eyes took me in.

"I don't want you getting into a fight."

Over me. Even I didn't have enough ego to voice it.

Reed's eyes intensified as though confused.

"I don't like the idea of...people getting hurt over..." *Oh, drat, I am floundering.* "I don't want you to get hurt over something so..."

Seeing me struggle, Reed leaned in, halting my rambling. "You don't want me to fight for you?"

Did he want to fight?

I couldn't think with him this close. I had the biggest crush on Reed.

"Why would you?" I managed to whisper.

His brows rose fractionally as though incredulous I'd even ask such a thing.

I could only murmur. "I don't understand. I just didn't want to see you hurt."

Something unguarded flickered in Reed's eyes as they softened momentarily. He clearly hadn't expected that response. His hand shifted to cup the side of my neck, thumb brushing the dangle of my earring.

A hint of wry amusement filled his expression, though he found my concern for his well-being laughable.

"What are you doing here tonight?"

I lifted my chin at his censuring tone, taking in the press of his full lips, drawing into a slight frown, brows furrowed. How did I even begin to answer that?

"You haven't been here in a while," Reed murmured.

I want to get laid.

Preferably by a man who looks and smells like you. Do you have a brother?

I deflected. "A girl's not allowed to have a drink and enjoy her Friday night?" *Or her birthday.*

His head tipped in that subtle way that really shouldn't have looked effortless. "It's Sunday."

Drat. His hand fell from my neck to brace against the back of the chair, and I immediately missed the contact.

Keeping track of the date often proved challenging in my unconventional lifestyle—the not-so-glamorous hustle of an influencer rarely adhered to regular business hours or anything resembling a routine.

He dipped his head, brushing my ear.

"How much have you had to drink?"

I clenched my thighs instinctively, my palm lifting to press against the firm wall of his jacketed chest. Instead of pushing him away, I seemed to anchor myself to his solid presence.

"I'm fine, I just—"

"How much?" His dubious expression made it clear he didn't believe me for a second.

Avoiding his searing stare, I glanced toward the remnants of my drinks. "Three?"

Reed's mouth ticked up at the corners, a rueful amusement dancing in his eyes.

"If you plan on staying here all night, lightweight, you'll have me for company."

My eyes widened, bristling at the gentle jab as a frisson of heated awareness licked through me at the implication of him staying by my side all night.

"Lightweight?" I echoed, indignant.

Reed grinned, his tongue darting out a little between his teeth as he leaned against the bar top.

"You're like Bambi on ice when you drink," he murmured, eyes dancing with mirth. I could only see his tongue and felt my entire body respond to that.

I could hear my governess in my head. Ladies do not daydream of being taken like a wild woman by a man like this.

I gasped, affronted. "I'm appalled by your candor. I can absolutely hold my weight—"

"Even when you're offended, you're still so..." His achingly sensual smile only widened as I sputtered.

"Articulate?" I supplied, arching a brow.

"Proper," Reed countered, that Northeastern accent rendering the simple word into something indecently sensual as it rolled off his tongue.

A weighted beat stretched between us, the air thrumming with unvoiced tension. Reed's gaze seemed to search my face, his brow furrowing slightly as if piecing together a puzzle.

"How long did your family move you guys around?" he asked abruptly. "Kids usually have accents if they've been around another language until about thirteen or so."

I blinked, startled by his astute observation.

Memories of my childhood flashed through my mind.

The familiar streets of Chiswick, the rolling hills of Oxfordshire, occasional stints in America, and trips to Calcutta, which my parents took us on to preserve Mum's culture. My Mum's voice echoed in my ears, her soft accent a constant backdrop to our lives. A life I no longer had.

"I was a teenager..."

Reed nodded, his eyes never leaving mine. It was as if he was absorbing the information, tucking it away for future reference.

Reed tipped his head back, looking behind me, his eyes darkening.

"Are you going to do that cute little bow again when you thank me for saving you this time?"

My heart stuttered at the word "cute".

I fought to keep my composure, willing myself not to visibly react.

Do not combust. Do not move.

As his words fully registered, confusion swept through me." Save me from what?"

Legacy

CHAPTER ONE — EXCERPT

"Motherfucker."

Running across a rooftop at midnight to catch a criminal was not the way I wanted my Friday night to go down. Not exactly.

I was going to kill this motherfucker.

I leapt off the building I was in, the wind whipping in my hair, as I gained on the fucker running from me.

The skyline around me stretched out the lights guiding me towards my target. A maze of concrete that I knew would hurt if I splattered on it.

Street pizza was not what I wanted to be tonight.

Not when I was chasing a potential perp.

God, when I got my fucking claws and fangs into him—he'd scream for a completely different reason.

I was bolting down and right before he hit the next building, I caught him at the edge.

"Not so fast, fucker." It was a growl ripped from my throat as he elbowed me. With a snarl I had him on the ground. But he was a fighter.

He maneuvered in a way that I felt the elbow coming at my throat and ducked, landing on my back.

He took off, leaping over the edge. I shouted as I drew back and took the jump with him.

I thought he'd make it.

He kinda did, but he groaned as he hit the ground. I definitely made it the air whooshing from my lungs as I rolled smoothly.

Or I would've. I landed wrong.

I felt a searing pain in my shoulder that ripped right through me as I groaned. But my other hand moved. My gun yanking out as I took the shot.

With confidence. He groaned going down as I saw him get hit.

"Fuck!" I groaned dropping onto my knees. I shot him again taking him out as I heard someone land next to me.

"Boss, you good?"

Landon Donohue.

My right hand most of the time when I was working.

I looked up into dark eyes and darker hair whipping in the wind as another man dropped down next to him.

Derek Macall, shaved head, piercings and tattoos. My team. Sean was downstairs in the car.

I let out a breath.

"Straight." I would get Kieran to set it.

Three days later, Kieran did not in fact set it and the pain was getting too excruciating to ignore.

I couldn't. But I didn't wanna go to the hospital and deal with another presumptuous doctor or nurse ever again. But I couldn't stop myself.

Sean watched me one evening struggling to put my jacket on.

"Just ask for Nisha Graham when you go," he muttered. His clear blue eyes watched me wincing a little. "She's solid. Nicest lady there."

"Just because you got favorites, doesn't mean I trust them." I bit out. "You fuck her or something?"

He made a noise. "Nah, she's cool." Right. He just looked uneasy as I groaned about my shoulder. "Just go check it out tonight."

"Fine. I'll go."

"Nisha Graham." Sean repeated. "Trust me. She's good."

We'll see about that.

～

A cat photo from Kieran lit up my phone screen on the way to the hospital with Nisha.

It was of a chubby gray cat with a bandaged paw, frowning at the camera.

That's you.

Another photo appeared of a regal black cat with a crown rolling its eyes.

That's big bro.

I snorted.
I sent him back a photo of a tombstone.

Keep texting me annoying shit and this will be you.

BWahahah. Nice to see you getting on board the meme train.

Such a fucking idiot

You didn't fix my arm

I'm not a doctor

That was your first mistake with me

I groaned.
Little brother's fucking sucked sometimes.
Even if I loved the little shit.
Right now, my shoulder throbbing in pain?
I couldn't focus on anything else.

Such a shit

Go to the hospital, bro

Stroke of Temptation

CHAPTER ONE — EXCERPT

"Take the fucking shot, Grim."

Cole Kincade's voice came through my ear-piece.

The cold Minsk air in Belarus was never welcome against my skin as I pressed the rifle to my cheek.

This wasn't my first rodeo.

Not even close.

In the last three years? I had killed so many people. Death was a business where I came from now. And Talia Nash was not an easy teacher.

I dealt in it plenty enough. Dressed in all back, I knew nobody could see me.

If they did, they knew they were dead. My presence meant one of two things—one, they fucked up and they were going to die or two, they were already dead.

I didn't show up for good news or birthdays.

I should've felt at home on the rooftop. I should've been at peace with knowing it was yet another kill.

I felt nothing anymore.

After years of doing this? I hit twenty with a numbing agent across my chest from how many times I had done things that would've made a normal civilian throw up.

A shuddering breath left me as I was looking through my scope from the rooftop of the hotel I was on.

Staring down at the politician on the opposite side of the building. Currently trying to shoot his brother.

I let out an exhale in the twelve degree weather.

I fucking hated Europe in the winter. I hated winter in general. My breath fogged in the frigid air.

I forced my heart rate to slow down as I inhaled and exhaled.

My toes had gone numb an hour ago and now I wouldn't be surprised if Cole had to peel me off the fucking roof himself when I was done.

My target couldn't see me. But I could see him.

In the shadow of midnight I was the grim reaper.

But Cole was my partner on the other side oversight in tech watching cameras, handling surveillance.

He made sure nobody got to me. And in turn I executed everything according to plan.

Or I would. If I could take the shot.

"I swear to God, Grim—"

"I'm *trying*—" I growled. "Target is fighting with his brother—they're too close—"

"Have some fucking confidence," another voice growled. Caleb. Cole's twin brother. The two Aussies were former SAS and solely devoted to tech.

Both of them in my ear meant nothing but a fucking headache for me.

"Shut the fuck up—" I growled.

"Take the fucking shot—"

"You're a fucking pussy—"

I exhaled and turned off the ear piece.

Instead of hearing their voices I heard another in my ear.

In. Out. Breathe.

Breathe.

Breathe.

On your third exhale, take the shot, Thierry.

"I can't," I whispered. "I can't hurt innocents. His brother did nothing wrong."

Her voice appeared in my head. *Alma Nash.*

Current head of Talon. My former mentor. I should've felt something. Anything other than displaced.

My fingers trembled slightly.

I had done this nine thousand times. So why did I feel a calling for something other than this. In the distance, a flash of neon pink went off in another building.

I planted my feet wider. Bracing myself.

Take the shot on your third breath.

Have some confidence. You've done this before.

Several times.

Do not let your thoughts control you.

Breathe.

Take the shot, Reaper.

I exhaled slowly. And on the third exhale—I fired.

$$\backsim$$

"…Hung up on me," Cole was bitching. "That's what he fucking did."

I grinned as I got into the car at his disbelief. My cheeks hurt from the cold and from my laughter. His twin brother, Caleb laughed outright not bothering to hold back either.

"You are distracting as all fuck," I shot back climbing into the SUV as Caleb rolled his blue eyes at me. "I told you I could take the shot I needed *silence—*"

"You could've taken the shot without silence—" Cole sputtered.

"No, I couldn't—"

Yes, I could've. I was good at what I did. *Hence, Reaper One.*

In three years, Talia put me through brutal boot camp. A joke compared to what her father, Malcolm had taught her, but helpful.

I avoided Malcolm Nash like the plague. He didn't like my family because he didn't like his daughter with Andrei.

It didn't take me long to realize why Andrei was so livid.

Nobody knew about him and Talia.

Not Maxine, just me and Teo because Talia was like a Mom to us.

I knew bits and pieces about Andrei's relationship with Talia.

Bits and pieces enough to know—she loved him, he loved her, and her father hated my brother. By default, my entire family.

I had no fucking clue how Talia kept her secrets from him, but it seemed like on paper?

Malcolm trusted Talia enough to believe her. Leave her to her devices.

And I couldn't imagine what she had done to get there.

"If you took any longer taking the fucking target out, we'd both be sixty by now." Cole shot back turning around from the passenger side as Caleb, always the driver, took off into the night.

"Shut the fuck up—" I growled feeling irritation.

My headache was back and blossoming behind my eyes. I needed some food and some rest.

Anything to not feel...*whatever* I felt inside of my chest.

"I don't fucking understand how anyone tolerates you in their ear for longer than two minutes. *This* is why Samara tried to murder you in cold blood."

"Twice." Cole smiled as though he was proud for riling up our other team member.

Sitting in the backseat with my rifle I watched Caleb snort.

"Samara would murder anyone in cold blood," Caleb muttered. "She doesn't even need a reason. She'll just do it because she's bored."

"God, I love her bloodthirsty," Cole sighed.

I laughed. "If we tell her you said that she might actually kill you."

"I'd be honored." Cole was smitten. Sort of. I just think he liked her because she was sharp-tongued and lethal.

The entire unit I operated in was broken up into smaller teams.

The other two members of our team weren't out tonight, but that didn't mean anything.

They were handling the other half of the assignment back at the hotel we were in. And the unease was settling into my blood again.

I didn't understand why.

"She get the target yet?" I asked.

Cole started. "Well, if you didn't hang up on me, maybe I would've—"

"She did." Caleb cut in. The older of the two by a solid minute, it showed in his ability to constantly hand Cole his ass on a platter.

The twins were identical, six-feet one, over two hundred something pounds of pure blonde Australia. Save for one thing.

Everything below Cole's neck was completely tatted which was how I only knew the difference.

Otherwise?

They were the same person when they needed to be. And Cole might've taken all the personality from Caleb at birth.

I grinned at Cole's expression.

"Why do you two never let me finish?"

"Because you're an idiot." I said it at the same time as Caleb and he shot me a rare grin.

"I am not—"

"Shut up, Cole, it's four in the morning—" Caleb growled. "I'm starting to get a fucking headache from you."

"I'm just saying—" Cole wouldn't shut the fuck up.

I groaned covering my eyes, my cheeks spread in a grin.

I'd met them when I'd joined Talon years ago after Talia had taken me in. Talia was just as scary as she was nice. I'd spent my teenager years running wild and the nine hundred almost-felonies under my belt?

Andrei had gotten fed up and lost it. Talia had offered to train me.

With her family. Natasha, her sister, and their cousin Alma.

In three years? I didn't recognize myself. My first year had been brutal with Talia cutting off sugar and anything bad for me and my ADHD.

I watched the streets pass by as Caleb drove us back.

By the time we got back to the hotel I was tired, but we were flying out tonight. I needed to shower and change and get back to Cape Verde with my team.

Even if I felt that little niggle of something bothering me in the back of my mind.

Even if it was something I couldn't quite put my finger on.

Something I had been feeling for a while as I felt the jostle of the car as I tucked my colder hands into my pocket to feel—her.

I just couldn't put my finger on it. The neon pink lights flashed. Butterflies. They couldn't exist here in the cold, so someone turned them into signs. I squeezed around the object in my jacket I carried with me all the time.

I didn't take it out in the car in front of anyone though.

I felt my lips tip up even as I rubbed my chest.

We arrived the hotel adopted our disguises of European college kids and I put a hat on so nobody could even guess I wore contacts to mute out my face.

I always wore brown contacts with the Nash's and this way, nobody knew I was a DuPont, but Talia and her cousin Alma.

I always tucked myself into the shadows so nobody could find me.

"I think that sexy little blonde from earlier is texting me—" Cole stated but got cut off by his brother.

"You mean she's texting who she thinks you are. Remember Alma, doesn't want trouble," Caleb told him eyeing his brother with concern as we walked up casually into the back.

I shook my head at the two of them.

When we'd been younger I had gone through every woman imaginable.

Every. Woman. I. Could. And then something happened to me along the way.

I didn't know what.

I didn't know why.

But everything in my life felt off.

The numbers and letters on the elevator blurred. Nobody texted me because I didn't text.

And even if I felt my limitations weighing on me I was quiet in the elevator as the twins argued about which girl Cole was actually talking to.

They said something about me going with them but I shook my head. Caleb looked at me concerned but Cole dragged him off.

"Be ready to leave!" He shouted. I rolled my eyes walking into my room. The moment I was in the room, my hands drew out something I hadn't been able to throw away ever.

Not once. Not since I got it. For some fucking reason.

I didn't like nice girls. Sweet girls with pretty doe eyes and lush lips. The women I liked were experienced. But I was her first kiss.

I looked down at the pink butterfly hair pin. It looked like it belonged to an older woman when I'd glanced at it.

Not...her. I didn't know her name. Still.

Sure as fuck, wasn't about to start calling her Amelia.

But she was my good luck charm.

I had tucked it into my pocket and kept it that day. It had sat in my bedroom all week before Talia and I left.

Andrei didn't even look at me he was so livid with the war he was in now with his mother. I'd just held onto it the entire time.

Over the years I learned everywhere I carried it, I was safe.

The one time I didn't? I forgot it in my hotel room and I almost got blown up.

Since then, I took *that* pink butterfly clip with me everywhere. I set it on my bedside table aware if I even so much as laid down, she was back.

Sometimes *she* came into my thoughts. Invaded them.

I didn't understand why.

It was stupid. It was just a kiss. Andrei had kicked me out of New York. I shouldn't have thought about her.

But every so often, she snuck into my thoughts. Maybe because she caught me at a bad time because nobody else did.

Maybe because of her sexy voice and insulting me.

The DuPont men definitely had a type.

She reminded me of Talia a little. Giving me attitude. *Lip.* I bit back a grin tucking it into my pocket again.

She was a world away from me now.

And I'd never see her again.

~

We made it back to the Talon compound within forty-eight hours. Located in Cape Verde, Africa.

Immediately my body sighed at being hit with the sweltering heat.

"Never get used to that heat," he grumbled swearing up a storm. I liked it here. Or I had.

Lately, I didn't like it anywhere.

This wasn't the kind of place civilians showed up in. No.

Not unless they had a death wish.

I didn't know how Malcolm Nash, Talia's father got his start in life, but art security private teams turning into black-ops killers had not been the reality I had been prepared for.

On paper that's what Talon was. Private security. In reality?

It was so much darker.

Once Malcolm had passed control to Talia, the unit had changed a lot, Talia driving a sword through the old guard and revamping the compound to a modern day structure inside an older temple like place.

It was an enormous structure all white stone and fortified. A labyrinth of hallways and bedrooms and split up. On either end were the two towers that oversaw the entire thing.

One belonged to Talia.

The other was empty and sometimes Alma liked to crash there but sometimes she went and kinda did her own thing.

"Carter and the she-devil herself arrived earlier," Caleb muttered to me. "They should be inside."

My grin was quick at the mention of Samara as his she-devil.

145

Samara wasn't bad per se.

But unlike Talia, Talon was all she had. And she took her job seriously. I didn't have a problem with Samara, but Carter I was partial too.

Bexley Carter was the other half of the IT team, on good terms with Cole and Caleb. The kid was nineteen with way too much potential to be sitting in Cape Verde.

She needed to get out a live a little—even if it felt like she already lived too much.

We barely made it inside before a striking five-eight brunette with her hair pulled into a braid at her back and all black on appeared.

Her outfit and her hair seemed to absorb all the light around her. Caleb muffled his groan into his fist.

"Samara," Cole grinned. Her features were sharp and her dark eyes tip-tilted and feline as she took us in.

"Alma wants you," she motioned to me ignoring him, her voice was low and smooth, with the hint of her English accent.

I wasn't sure where Samara was from but she was definitely mixed.

Nobody here had real identities.

Malcolm had a habit of picking up people who weren't really going to be seen again.

Samara happened to be one of them.

And now, she was Alma's right hand. She spoke for the head most of the time. And Bexley Carter was Alma's little pet. The two girls were closer to her and loyal to a fault.

But I didn't think Samara liked me very much.

I tipped my head to Samara, not because I didn't care to speak to her, my schedule was thrown out of wack, and my headache was back.

Following behind her I watched Cole and Caleb give each other a loaded look as I left.

Those idiots.

I always thought while Caleb dreaded Samara, Cole was into the kind of woman who could kill him with a few words.

His eyes lit up whenever he saw her. and right now he was definitely checking out her ass.

I gave him the finger leaving the foyer entirely as we made our way through the hall and I heard a smothered chuckle from them.

"How's Natasha?" I asked her after a moment of silence. Samara didn't want to talk.

Then again, I wasn't her favorite person. I was close to everyone and Samara despised being near anyone save for Alma who she obeyed like God.

"Good."

Got it.

Natasha had been in an accident on one of her assignments.

Her right leg had been injured and she hadn't really recovered fully but I also thought it might've been because of the way Malcolm pushed his girls—she hadn't been able to recover.

She took me up the stairs and into Alma's tower, and motioned for me to head on up without looking at me.

"And Talia?"

"Good."

Got it. End of conversation.

Taking a deep breath I walked up the steps to Alma's space the cooler breeze coming from above letting me know her windows were open.

Inside, the circular room, with white light, billowing white curtains and windows all around—I was momentarily blinded.

Alma was at her perch when I walked in from her seat by the window.

She always liked it there staring at the expanse of sea and the church up ahead in her short white dresses.

I had met Alma years ago when Talia had brought me in as a rowdy teenager and unlike the other Talon operatives who took one look at me and scowled—she had taken me in and been kinder.

She had said I reminded her of her brother who had passed away and she wanted to right by him.

Alma stood to her full five-four and slender self, her black hair flowing around her olive toned body, almond shaped eyes dark and focused on me, long lashes fanning out over her high cheekbones.

She raised an arched brow at me and smiled wide. *Still scary.*

I knew Alma had a heart of gold and she was friendly, but Alma was the kind of frightening otherworldly beautiful you had to suspend your reality for. Spooky. Eerie. Downright scary.

The air around her dipped and shifted. Dropping a few temperatures.

But by now I got used to it, her doll-like features highlighted by those dark fathomless eyes.

She was gorgeous in a way Samara wasn't.

But both of them were a little terrifying. Then again, Talia and Natasha were also so I guess that ran in the genes.

"You wanted me?"

She smiled a little. "Sit."

She motioned to her window sill. She often read there and hung out. I didn't know how Alma came to Talon. Only that Talia rescued her like she did the others.

Now Alma was at the top of the pyramid.

"How are you?" She murmured.

Her words had a musical lilt to them and she rolled her r's all the time to my teasing and I figured she might be Latin.

"You don't look so good."

Her eyes watched me carefully.

I resisted the urge to say anything contrary to that. Of course she would know.

"I ask because Talia is not doing good, and I think she needs a break." Alma sat with me and tucked her knees to her chest.

"Not doing good, how?" Now I was worried. Talia was the love of my older brother's life. If anything happened to her? He would burn everything to the ground.

"Not sure..." Alma spoke softly and I heard her out. "Maybe she needs to go see your brother." Alma definitely figured it out when she saw me which wasn't surprising. Talia would tell her about Andrei.

"I can go check on her," I offered. "Andrei would be pissed if anything happened."

She nodded looking out to the sea. "Malcolm will be here in a few days. You need to stay out of his way."

Yikes. That never bode well for anyone.

Not that he was awful. I mean, he was. But nobody could live up to his standards and when he was here?

Alma and I had to pretend to be invisible. Because nobody really knew Alma led the teams. Everyone thought Talia still did.

There were too many secrets across Talon.

And I was one of them.

"If I need you, I'll call." Her eyes met mine searching my face. "You do not look good."

No. I didn't feel good.

But I couldn't put my finger on it.

One week later, I felt the moment she was in my room.

Years of being trained let me know when something was happening. The unease had vanished from days ago, but now it resurfaced.

"Wake up, Thierry. You need to leave."

My eyes opened to Alma in my face.

Dark eyes. Raven hair. Olive skin. Ghostly in the moonlight she looked unreal and frightening in the dark like a wraith appearing.

She had always been a little scary, but tonight more so than ever while jarring me awake.

"You need to take Talia and leave the country. Vamos!"

She was saying something in Spanish I didn't understand.

But then again, I barely spoke proper English with her.

I knew when Alma started speaking Spanish though shit had hit the fan.

Hence, why at three in the morning she was in my room. Talon compound wasn't known for being a place that made noise.

It wasn't known for being the kind of place you freaked out in. No, it was a fortified tower of discretion.

No loud noises. No disruptions.

Years of training kicked in as Alma gripped my face forcing me to focus on her ghostly eerie appearance.

I couldn't deny she was beautiful, but in a way that was a little frightening, with her too sharp features and wild eyes.

"W-what—"

"Malcolm is *dead*. Talia is pregnant. You must take her to Andrei. Tonight. Now."

My brain felt like it was going to explode. *Malcolm was dead? What the fuck? Talia was—Malcolm was supposed to be visiting.*

Who killed him?

It was only logical explanation.

"Are you insane?"

Dark, void-like eyes watched me.

When I first met Alma, she made no noise and she was a little terrifying when I got close to her. And it took a lot to scare me.

There was nothing in her eyes.

Like there was no life in them.

Pitch black and I knew anyone who met her in the dark was meeting their worst nightmare. But I loved her as my mentor and the few people in life who knew how to handle me.

The room went frightening arctic.

"Focus. You need to leave tonight—"

"W-why? What?" I was a little dazed. "What do you mean Malcolm is dead? *Who killed him?"*

Alma didn't answer me she just grabbed my face and looked at me with her spooky eyes.

"I told you years ago, if anything happened to threaten your happiness, I will defend it with my life. You are my second chance to do what I couldn't do in my past life. Do not fail me. Take your sister-in-law and leave—tonight. Otherwise, people will die. And one of them will be her."

She didn't need to tell me twice. Alma had told me years ago her loyalty to me was one to Talia, and for her brother who had died years ago.

Alma said I looked just like him and she wanted to right by him.

I nodded dumbly as I leapt up out of bed my head still aching and spinning.

"When am I leaving?"

She tossed me my shirt noticing I was in my briefs.

"Now."

Authors Note

Thank you so much for accomplishing the Titan Security Mission.

My initial goal was to write Titan Security, Underworld Kings, & Midnight Gods.

I couldn't have asked for a better series, but it's time to say goodbye to everyone at Titan.

Thank you so much for reading all of my books.

I didn't imagine anyone would enjoy or like my work. Or love it so much.

But this will be final book.

Thank you

Lilah

About the Author

Lilah Lance writes romance for all the girls who dream of being seen, being *accepted*, and being loved for *who they are*.

Get exclusive content and giveaways by signing up for Lilah's newsletter on http://lilahlance.com where you can get sneak peeks and news before anyone else.